Stories by M.T. Bass

MOTHERLESS CHILDREN

MURDER BY MUNCHAUSEN BOOK #4

BY

M.T. BASS

AN ELECTRON ALLEY PUBLICATION

MUDCAT FALLS, U.S.A.

Electron Alley Corporation
The Herald Building
732 Broadway Avenue
Lorain, OH 44052

Manufactured in the United States of America

Edited by Elizabeth N. Love

ISBN 978-1-946266-20-0 (Trade Paperback)
ISBN 978-1-946266-19-4 (eBook)
ISBN 978-1-946266-21-7 (Audio Book)

www.mtbass.net

For Tom W.

The Three Laws

1. A civilian-owned and operated synthetic humanoid entity may not act in any manner so as to engage in or cause any harmful or offensive contact against a human being or, through inaction, allow a human being to come to harm.

2. A civilian-owned and operated synthetic humanoid entity must obey the directives and orders given it by human beings except in those instances where such directives and orders would conflict with the First Law.

3. A civilian-owned and operated synthetic humanoid entity may protect its own existence as long as such protection does not conflict with the First or Second Laws.

Federal Technology Administration Regulations

"Hope we're not just the biological boot loader for digital super-intelligence. Unfortunately, that is increasingly probable."

"With artificial intelligence, we are summoning the demon."

~Elon Musk

Barcodes

"Why did they call *us?*" EC asked as he walked up.

Wally looked down at his fellow detective. "I dunno. Dead body? Ya think?" He nodded towards the corpse sprawled out on the pavement in the alley.

"But why us? Was he Munchausened?"

"He was barcoded."

"Like the others?"

"I ain't scanned him yet. You want to do the price check?"

EC looked up at Wally grinning back down at him.

"So, where's Jake?" Wally asked.

"DC. It's Wyatt's birthday."

"So, you and me then, eh?"

"You got the scanner?" EC asked.

"Just waiting for you, man." Wally lifted the yellow crime scene tape and they ducked under.

They stood back from the body as the Bunny Suit boys got their pictures.

"Where's the code?" EC asked.

"Lower back. Like the others," said one of the CSI techs.

"You know…" Wally cocked his head to one side, then to the other. "I know this guy."

"How's that?" EC asked.

Wally leaned over and snapped a shot with the camera on

his phone. He started the search program. "I know this guy."

"You know everyone."

"Damn near."

"He's all yours," said the CSI tech.

"Any ID?" EC asked. He looked at Wally watching the screen of his phone.

"Stripped clean, again. This one's a bit different. A little too…you know, made up. Fresh haircut. Looks like a manicure to me. The shoes are five hundred a pair. He didn't get those at Goodwill."

"Strangulation?"

"Looks like it. Quick and dirty. No struggle," Wally said.

"Can you guys roll him over? Let me get the scan."

Two of the Bunny Suit Boys turned the body to the right. One lifted the back of his t-shirt. Just above the belt line was a tattooed bar code.

EC knelt down and took a shot with his phone. "Thanks."

"Not much else for us to do."

"Don't suppose there were any witnesses."

"Maybe the cameras, but not likely. The alley's off the way. I doubt there's an angle on them from outside," said the Bunny Suit Boy. "Not likely there's any back here—not any that are working. It's a lovers lane…sort of."

"Great," said EC.

"Damn it," Wally said.

"What have you got?"

Wally held out his phone.

"That looks like the guy. You know him?"

Wally took his phone and scrolled the picture out. He showed it again to EC.

EC shook his head. "Damn it."

"What?" asked the CSI tech. "Who is he?"

"Did you dust everything in the alley?"

"Well, I mean—"

"And run his prints right away."

"I just wanted to do my job," Wally said wearily. "I don't need this."

"Who is he?" asked one of the Bunny Suit Boys.

"Looks like the Senator's son," EC said.

"Oh…"

"Yeah. *Oh.*" Wally shook his head. "I'll let you call downtown."

"Great."

"What did the scan say?"

EC ran the program. "I don't know what all the other numbers mean," EC said. "But he's definitely number three."

"Number three for what?"

"Damn it all, anyway." EC dialed downtown to Lt. Sands' office. "He's not going to be happy either."

"It's getting to be a big club," Wally said.

~~~

Wally and EC were done with the crime scene by the time Lt. Sands showed up. EC leaned against the front quarter panel of his cruiser staring at the body. Wally stood with the Bunny Suit Boys talking about the Browns' game.

"You sure it's him?" Lt. Sands came up to EC and leaned next to him.

"Yeah. The prints came back. It's him."

"Everybody done here?"

"I had them dust all the trash cans and dumpsters in the alley. There's a mess of prints, but I don't think they'll mean much."

"How's he working out?" Lt. Sands pointed to Wally.

"So far, so good."

Wally noticed Sands and came over from the CSI van. "Hey, Lieu. How's it going?"

"Another day in paradise, I guess. You?"

"I was doing well, you know, until Junior, here, made his appearance."

"No media?"

"Kept it off the radio. For now," EC said.

They walked over to the body.

"What is he, thirty?" asked Sands.

"Twenty-nine. Younger than the others," Wally said. "No wife. No kids."

"Same marks?"

Wally bent down, rolled him over and pulled up his shirt. "Same marks. Definitely number three."

Sands shook his head. "Get him out of here. Quick. And keep the barcode out of the news."

EC waved over the Coroner's men. "Nobody cares. That's what I like. It's kind of quiet. Almost peaceful."

"Not no more, it won't be," Wally stood back and let the men bag the body and put it on the stretcher.

"I'll need you there when I tell him," Sands said. "Just no mention of, you know, the Munchausen stuff."

"Maybe Jake—"

"He'll be back next week. I checked and the Senator's in town. So, we go over there this morning. Get back to the house and put on ties and jackets. I'll talk to the Captain, then we'll head over."

Wally and EC watched Lt. Sands walk back to his car.

"So, how does it feel to be the lead detective?" Wally asked.

"Me? You were here first."

"You're the old pro, man. Captured the Baron and everything. I think it's you. I'm just a nobody."

"Yeah, well, where's Jake when you really need him?"

"Come on. It'll be fun."

EC glared at Wally.

"You know, dead bodies and all?"

"Yeah. Dead bodies and all."

~~~

The Senator

They waited in the front hallway of the Senator's Bratenahl mansion.

"Must be nice," Wally said to EC, inspecting the palatial entryway

Lt. Sands gave him a scowl.

EC stared down the hall and out the back window to Lake Erie pushing in towards the shore. He nodded. "Yeah."

"Just let me talk, okay?" Sands said.

"You're the boss, boss." Wally shoved his hands into his pants pockets.

A woman came around the corner. She was dressed in a conservative business suit and clutched a leather binder. "Lt. Sands?"

Sands stepped forward.

"Is this really necessary?" She did not reach out with her hand.

"It is. The Safety Director called, right?"

She nodded. "What is this about?"

"We really need to speak with the Senator and his wife this morning."

"Well, he is very busy."

"I understand."

Sands, Wally, and EC gave her the bad cop look.

"Very well. Come this way." She led them down the hall and off to the left. In the back corner was an office with tall windows facing out onto the lake. "He'll be in momentarily. He will need to leave shortly for a meeting."

"I understand." Sands stared at the woman without an expression on his face. "We'll wait here."

The woman nodded and left.

The room was dark, lined with book cases, some filled with books, but most held a collection of items and photos from twenty-plus years in politics. A desk was positioned in front of them at the window. A pair of loveseats faced one another at the other end of the room.

It seemed like a much longer wait than it was. Ten minutes later, Senator Scofield and his wife came into the room. She sat down quickly on one of the sofas. He paced around behind his desk.

Wally held the Chief-of-Staff outside, then quietly closed the door.

The Senator noticed.

Sands saw that he looked older than on video feeds. No makeup, he decided. His hair grayer, not so sandy-colored.

EC wandered to the other side of the sofas.

Wally stood by the door and watched the Senator closely the entire time.

Senator Scofield shuffled a few papers around on his desk, then looked at Sands. "I—I have a meeting…"

"Senator…please," Sands said softly. He motioned for him to join his wife on the loveseat.

"No. What is it?"

Sands turned so he could see them both. "Your son,

Mitchell, was found earlier this morning—"

"Is he all right?" asked Mrs. Scofield.

Sands looked at her. "I'm sorry, ma'am. He was found dead."

"Dead?" asked the Senator. *"Dead?"*

"Yes, sir. He appears to have been murdered."

Wally and EC watched them closely.

Mrs. Scofield stared straight ahead, then bowed her head.

The Senator sat down at this desk. "How?"

"He has been taken downtown. We'll know much more later."

"How?"

"We are not exactly sure, sir," Sands lied. "It is still very early."

"And these guys?" Senator Scofield asked.

"They are the detectives handling the case. They work for me."

"Where was he found?"

"He was found in an alley in the AsiaTown District."

"What happened?"

"Senator…"

Mrs. Scofield got up and walked around behind the desk. She stood next to the Senator, put her hand on his shoulder, and stared out the window.

The Senator picked up a paper, then put it down again. He took a deep breath, then exhaled slowly.

"I am very sorry to bring this news to you and Mrs. Scofield." Lt. Sands realized that this would be their public reaction. He took out a business card. He slid it in front of the Senator. "There are…details that will need to be addressed. If you or your

Chief-of-Staff can call me, I'm sure we can arrange to take care of them quietly."

Mrs. Scofield crossed her arms.

The Senator never looked up. "Yes. Yes, of course."

"We'll see ourselves out," said Sands.

Wally opened the door. The Chief-of-Staff was there listening through the door. Her face was drawn out.

Sands handed her another business card. "We'll need to have the body ID'd. And we'll have a few questions. It would be best to see them downtown soon."

She took the card.

"We know the way out."

Sands, Wally, and EC walked by her to the front entrance.

Wally glanced back to see her standing in the hallway, waiting to go in.

'It's a different world," Sands said as they got in the Crown Vic. "A different world."

"But it all ends the same way," said Wally.

~~~

The Cruiser

Lt. Sands sat staring down the long driveway leading back to Lakeside Road. He did not start the car. "What do we know about these guys?"

EC exchanged a glance with Wally in the back seat.

"This kid is the third one, so far," Wally said.

"Patterns?" Sands asked.

"All we know for sure is the barcodes imprinted on their backs," EC said.

"What do they mean?"

"You know, we could use some help. Some real help," EC said. "Sorting out what the numbers mean."

Sands winced. "The Geeks can't help?"

"Keyboard tappers," Wally said. "Tell them what to do and they'll do it. Not much imagination."

"Yeah, well, imagination got Q in trouble that last time," Sands said.

Wally shrugged and looked back at the three-story mansion. "The Senator's going to want some answers. Sooner rather than later, I'm assuming."

"There's a link there—in the numbers. It would help to know for sure what they mean," EC said.

They sat for a long time, looking at the lake.

Wally started whistling softly.

Sands scowled in the rearview mirror.

"Sorry. Force of habit, I guess."

"And there's no connection between the vics?" Sands asked.

"I'm sure there is, but what it is…" EC said. "The numbers would help."

Wally started whistling again.

Sands squinted back.

"Sorry."

"I can't get him his job back," Sands said.

"Maybe he could consult or something," EC said.

"Would he do it?" Sands asked.

"Jake would know," EC said. "He'd be your best bet."

"When does he get back?"

"Monday."

"You want him, too. Right?" Sands asked.

EC nodded.

Sands looked back at Wally.

"Yeah. Sure. The more the merrier as far as I'm concerned."

"Tell Jake to talk to Q. Let's get some help on this," Sands said, starting the car. "Low key for now, but make some headway quick before the Senator asks for a task force or something."

EC and Wally just nodded.

Sands pulled away for the station house.

~~~

Lost Souls

Jake climbed the back stairs to his apartment. The door was unlocked and it gave him pause.

He reached for his Colt 1911 and drew, setting down his duffle bag. The door slid open quietly and he stepped inside. Dark at his end of the hall, he moved quietly in towards the front, clearing the laundry room and the bathroom at the back.

He heard dishes clinking in the kitchen. He moved along the wall that way, clearing the bedrooms along the way quickly.

"I can hear you out there," came from the kitchen. "And put your gun away, already."

Q.

Jake put his pistol in its holster and retrieved his duffle bag, tossing it into the bedroom.

"How was DC?" Q asked. He sat at the table drinking a beer, sliding through pages on his iSlate. "What do you feed this cat, anyway?"

"He has eclectic tastes." Jake grabbed a beer from the fridge. "Not Chinese, that's for sure. I think Italian is his favorite."

"Like what?"

Jake leaned against the counter. "Penne pasta. Pizza. Chicken Parm, Lasagna."

"I didn't see any of that in there."

A black cat sat between them, following their conversation.

"How is she?"

Jake drank and nodded. "Good. It's all good—after a fashion."

"You moving to DC any time soon?" Q looked up at Jake.

He shook his head. Jake thought of Maddie and Wyatt. He started to say something, then just took another drink of Shiner Bock.

"Good. There's work to be done."

"Might be quicker to buy a lottery ticket, you know."

"I didn't say this would be quick. Besides, isn't the chase the thing for you?" Q asked.

"Four hundred million would be better. I've got big plans for this place, you know."

"Yeah. Right." Q shook his head. "I talked to EC. He said they're going to ask you to ask me to come back to work."

"*Really?*"

"Consulting job, I guess. They've got some bodies piling up. It'll be just like the good old times, Jake. On the hunt for bad guys, again."

"Bad guys?"

"There are always bad guys behind every Munchausen. You know that."

Jake nodded.

"And, *then*...

Jake looked at Q.

Q swung his iSlate around. "There are some bank accounts I need to take a look at. They'll be much easier to get to from the inside."

"Still chasing the dream, huh."

"It's out there, Jake. You know the Baron hid it somewhere

safe and we just have to find it and move it into our own safe little space in Switzerland or the Cayman Islands."

"And the lawyers who lost it in the first place?"

"You going to tell them?"

Jake smiled. He shook his head.

"Then who's to know?"

"You want pizza?"

"Sure. Why not."

"What about you?" Jake asked Frank the Cat.

Frank the Cat laid down on the floor, waiting.

~~~

Detective Kim

Jake and Q sat in the chairs across from Lt. Sands' desk watching him scribble out the paperwork.

EC sat on the couch next to Wally.

Wally scanned his iPhone.

Lt. Sands turned the paperwork around and slid it towards Q.

"Do I really need to read all of this?" Q asked.

"I don't see why," Lt. Sands said wearily. "You're just going to break all the rules anyway. Right?"

"Yeah. You're right." Q signed the consulting agreement. He pushed it back. "Great to be back on the team, again."

"Well, what in the hell are you waiting for? Everybody out of here…" He pointed at Jake. "Except for you."

EC stood up. He winked at Jake, shrugged his shoulders, then left.

"You're on your own," Q said, following EC out.

Wally was staring at his phone.

Lt. Sands cleared his throat.

"Oh, are we done here?" Wally asked.

"Yeah…I'll catch up with you guys in a minute," Jake said.

Lt. Sands motioned Wally to close the door.

"How is Maddie doing?" Lt. Sands asked.

"Good. Real good. Rising FBI star and all of that, you know. More of a desk job, though. And lots of PowerPoint presentations.

I'd hate it."

Lt. Sands nodded. "You're going to keep an eye on Q, right?"

"He'll be fine. What harm can he do?"

Lt. Sands shook his head. "I don't want to know."

"And so it shall be."

"Well, I've got another job for you."

"What's that?"

Lt. Sands picked up his phone and made a call. "Yeah, send her in."

"Her?"

"New blood."

"Oh, no. Why me?"

"Come on. It'll be…*fun.*"

Lt. Sands waved someone into his office.

"Really? Me?" Jake asked.

Lt. Sands stood up and smiled. "Yeah, *you.*"

A tall, young Asian woman entered the room.

Jake looked up.

"I—I've…I—" She looked at Lt. Sands. "Him?"

"Jake, this is Detective Kim." Lt. Sands smiled. "She's joining the Artificial Crimes Unit."

"Her?" Jake stood up. "Really?"

"He's just an old grouch, sometimes," Lt. Sands said. He winked at Jake. "Don't pay him any mind."

Detective Kim crossed her arms over her chest. She cocked her head and gave Jake an up-and-down look like he was a perp.

"What about EC?" Jake asked.

"He seems to be getting along pretty well with Wally since you've been gone."

"I don't know about this," Detective Kim said.

"Come on, guys, it'll be a blast." Lt. Sands sat back down behind his desk. He started shuffling papers. "Now, go out there and solve some crimes already."

Jake growled and left.

"But…"

"You better catch up with him," Lt. Sands said.

Detective Kim shook her head and chased after Jake. She asked, "Where are you going?"

"To get some lunch." He pressed the button for the elevator.

"But it's nine-thirty in the morning."

"Okay. Then breakfast." Jake got on and held the door. "You coming? If not…"

Kim ran to get on the elevator as the doors started to close.

Jake drifted into a back corner.

Kim stood, staring at the door. "Listen, I—"

"Not here. Not now."

She nodded and looked down at the floor.

They left the front door of the station and headed the three blocks over to Cutty's Deli.

Jake held the door open for Kim.

As they walked by the counter, Cutty stopped slicing and stared at Kim.

"Come on. This way." Jake led her to a back booth. "Sit here."

Jake went and got two cups of coffee from the counter.

"Thank you," Kim said when he got back.

Jake slid in across from Kim. He took a sip of coffee and glanced over at Cutty, who was staring them down. He shook his head. He held his hand up to keep him back.

Kim stared down into her coffee mug. Her straight black hair was cut much shorter now, to her shoulders, but still parted in the middle. She wore a maroon sweater with a gold blazer.

"I didn't know it would be you," she said.

"Why are you dressed like that?"

"What?" Kim looked up.

"You look like a realtor."

"I wanted to dress nice, okay? First day and all."

"Uh-huh."

"So, what? Is it casual Tuesday around here?"

Jake slowly shook his head. "Are you bringing any baggage with you?"

Kim locked eyes with Jake, unsmiling. "I really didn't have much choice."

"I don't know…"

"Look, it was either let myself get sucked into that clown-car operation on the east side—when I found out, I tried to get the hell out of there, but…"

"But Internal Affairs?"

"My back was against the wall and it started going the wrong way, fast. What would you have done?"

Jake shrugged.

"I know you've been pressed hard by those guys before."

"I didn't turn on anybody." Jake looked Kim in the eye.

"They had wiretaps going already," Kim said.

"And IAB came to you and said, look, you're either with us or against us, right?"

"I was not going to jail. I didn't do anything. But they threw a bad stink on me, too."

"And six guys took a fall in narcotics."

"They were bad guys, Jake."

"So they used you and now they've booted you out and over here."

"Yeah. Like you."

"…like me." Jake nodded.

"I got no friends in IA."

"It rubs people the wrong way, you know?" Jake nodded towards Cutty behind the counter. "We don't want any trouble around here, okay?"

"Well, they didn't give me a nice promotion and a desk in Robbery/Homicide. I'm chasing stupid robots now."

"I don't know. It might grow on you."

"I doubt it."

"Well, then, there's always being a mall cop." Jake smiled.

"Then I wouldn't have bailed on IA."

"No baggage, then?"

Kim shook her head.

"It'll take some time."

"It always does, doesn't it?" Kim gave him a half-smile. "We okay?"

"We'll see." Jake winked. "So, what do you want for breakfast? My treat."

~~~

Numbers

"So, where's my office?" Q asked.

"Office? Hey, pal, you see any offices around here?" Wally asked.

"Wow…it's kind of grim over here on this side." Q looked around the cop side of Exit Alley. The drab green walls were already flecking off peels of paint. "Maybe I could work over on the other side."

"You are working over here," said EC. "That way Jake can keep an eye on you."

"On me? Whatever for?"

"Come on." Wally led him back to the conference room. He held open the door. "In here."

EC flipped on the lights. There were the beginnings of a murder board against the far end. There were three BMV photographs taped to the top of the whiteboard.

"So, this is for real?" Q asked.

"Looks like it," Wally said, plopping himself down in a chair.

EC shut the door. "It's low-key for now."

Q walked over to the board and started reading the notes beneath the pictures of the three men.

ALAN BURR, 42, March 27, Warehouse District.

PAUL WHISTLER, 38, May 5, Edgewater Park.

MITCHELL SCOFIELD, 29, June 18, AsiaTown.

"Hey, isn't that—"

"Yup. The Senator's son," Wally said.

"Like I said, low-key for now, please," EC reminded Q.

Beneath the age, date of death, and location were blown-up pictures of barcodes. Numbers were scrawled out beneath them: 1 62355 87711 7, 3 89842 37729 4, and 2 58419 00621 8.

"None of those codes are in the GTIN database," EC said.

Q looked over each of the numbers again and thought for a moment. "Those last numbers are all wrong. They're mathematical check codes, but they don't compute out correctly."

"What's that mean?" asked Wally.

"Add up the odd numbers, multiply by three and add them to the even numbers. Drop everything but the ones digit. If it's not zero, then subtract it from ten and that's your check digit."

Wally looked at EC. "What's that mean?"

"Look, take the first bar code." Q pointed at the board, touching every other number. "One-plus-two-plus-five-plus-eight-plus-seven-plus-one is twenty-four. Times three is seventy-two. Then add up six-three-five-seven-and-one and you get twenty-two. Add seventy-two and twenty-two and you get ninety-four. Ten minus four is six. The check digit should be six, not seven."

"Okay…"

"The second check digit should be eight and not four. The third one should be six, not eight."

"So, what's that mean?" Wally asked.

"They're not legit barcodes."

"And that's your job here: figure out what those damn numbers mean," EC said.

"Doesn't look like location data—no lats and longs in there," Q said.

"Yeah, we thought about that," said Wally.

"But you're definitely thinking there is some kind of code going on here."

"That's why the Department is paying you the big bucks, right?" Wally asked.

"Yeah. Right. We're all in on this gravy train together," said Q.

"Well, what do you need?" EC asked.

"A laptop would be helpful."

"I'll requisition one."

"Top of the line. Intel, if you please."

EC shook his head. "You'll get what you get."

"So, what do you think is the deal with the Senator's son on this list?" Q asked.

"I don't want to know." Wally shook his head. "Sounds like nothing but trouble, any way you look at it."

"Any connection between the other two guys?" Q asked.

"Nothing but the bar codes, so far," EC answered. "Burr was a CPA. Whistler ran a restaurant down in Ohio City. No connections though—so far."

"And then the Senator's son…That seems a bit out of place."

"Yeah, and I'm sure it's going to kick this thing into high gear. So, we've got to get ahead of it."

"And they were all strangled, right?" Q asked.

"Seems like it was quick, too quick for human hands," Wally said. "Do you know how hard it is to actually squeeze the life out of someone? It doesn't go that easy."

"And so they're saying Munchausens, then."

"You catch on quick," Wally said.

"Anything on the Atlas grid."

"Nothing unaccounted for," said EC.

"A good old-fashion mystery then."

"I'll get the laptop," EC said. "Make yourself at home."

EC went out.

"You think you can crack this one?" Wally asked.

"Eventually."

"Well, the sooner the quicker, and then we'll all be happy to have the Senator go back to DC."

Q looked over the bar codes again.

"So, hop to it."

Q looked back at Wally.

"Come on now, son. You're the Wonderkin." Wally gave him a big smile. "Aren't you?"

~~~

AsiaTown

"You have got to be kidding me," Kim said.

"What?" asked Jake as he pulled his black Mustang convertible up next to the alleyway.

"AsiaTown?"

"Yeah. What?"

Kim grumbled to herself as she brushed the hair out of her face.

"It's where EC and Wally found the Senator's kid. Don't go politically correct on me either. We have some murders to solve."

"And who drives a car like this?"

"It's a classic."

Kim mumbled under her breath. She pushed open the door and got out, still fussing with her hair.

Jake smiled. "I'm not even going to ask."

"Where was the body?"

Jake got out and walked over to the alleyway entry. He stared down the way. "There. Next to the dumpster."

Kim stepped in and stooped down where Wally and EC found the Senator's son. "It's really him, huh."

"Do you think he was done here or dumped here?"

"How would I know?" Kim said.

"You're a detective, right?"

Kim mumbled again.

"Is that Mandarin?"

Kim looked up at Jake. *"Wèishéme shì, shì de."*

Jake smiled. *"Ránhòu, jiancè."*

Kim frowned. "I hate you already."

"Well, as a *detective* myself, I'd *detect* that he was dumped here."

"Why is that?"

Jake shrugged. "Too neat, you know? No fuss, no muss. No scuff marks. No thrashing about and such. And all the trash was still neatly in place."

"Yeah, I guess."

"You got your iSlate?"

"No. Where's yours?"

Jake scowled. "Never mind."

"Is that the way the others were? Were they moved?"

"No." Jake scratched his chin. "No, they weren't."

"So, what's that mean?"

Jake turned around and looked up and down the street.

Kim stood up. "So, now what?"

"Do you want to eat?"

"What? We just had breakfast. I can't eat again."

"But you know some good places to chow down around here, right?"

Kim scowled.

"Come on. Let's go check out the shops in the Plaza."

"What do you think we're going to find?"

"Maybe I need some chopsticks or something. Don't be a smart alec. Come on. It'll be fun—or do you want to go hang around the office?"

Jake headed to the Plaza with Kim in tow.

"Hey, wait for me."

Jake went into a shop. He nodded to the clerk behind the register and started looking at the knives in the counter.

"You need a blade?" asked Kim.

"No. Just browsing." Jake wandered down the long aisle, eyeballing the pottery and wall hangings. He turned and felt the fabrics of the gowns and blouses hanging from the racks in the back.

Kim followed him down the aisle and around.

"Xièxiè ni," Jake said as he headed out.

Kim nodded to the clerk, then caught up with Jake. "No chopsticks?"

"Don't you mock me."

"Who? Me?"

"So, do you know people down here?"

Kim nodded. "Why?"

"I don't think the Senator's son was moved far. I think he was killed down here. But why?"

"Random chance? What does AsiaTown have to do with Edgewater or the Warehouse District? That's where the other two guys were killed, right?"

"I don't know. I've got a hunch."

"Oh, good."

"Yeah? What have you got?"

"Nothing."

"So, do we go with the hunch or with what you've got?"

"Knock yourself out."

They wandered down the plaza stopping in the different shops and restaurants on their way to the grocery store at the far end. Jake went in and headed to the meat market in the back corner.

"What do you want?" the woman behind the counter asked

Jake brusquely. "Huh? What do you want?"

Jake smiled. "I've missed you, too, Lynn-Lee."

"And who is this?" Lynn-Lee pointed at Kim. "Is she with you? What happened to the redhead?"

"It's a long story."

"Fine. Don't tell me. I don't care. Now, what do you want?"

"Hmm, I don't know." Jake walked up and down the meat counter looking over the ribs and chops and poultry. He looked at Kim. "What do you think?"

"You want a duck?" asked Lynn-Lee, pointing to the whole birds hanging behind her by their feet. "They are fresh."

Kim started to say something but stopped.

"You—you there. Are you going to make this duck for this man?" Lynn-Lee asked.

"I—I—"

"Hey, go easy on her," Jake said.

"Yeah, yeah, yeah. I don't think she knows what to do with a duck." Lynn-Lee shook her head. "Not like the redhead."

Jake looked at Kim.

"I've done it…once."

"Let's just leave Maddie out of this. Okay?"

"Okay. What do you want? I don't have all day here." Lynn-Lee folded her arms over her chest.

Jake stepped up in front of Lynn-Lee and held up his phone with a picture of the Senator's son's face on it. "Him."

"Yeah. So?"

Jake scowled at her.

"I've seen him. He comes in sometimes. Not regular. Maybe once or twice a month."

"When was the last time?"

"Last week. Wednesday, maybe."

Jake looked at Kim.

"Are you sure it was Wednesday?" Kim asked.

"Yeah, yeah. Wednesday."

"What time?" Kim asked.

"I don't know. Maybe six o'clock." Lynn-Lee looked at Jake. "You should just buy a pork chop. Okay?"

"No," said Jake. "I want a duck."

"No, no, no. You get a pork chop. Okay?"

"Lynn-Lee…"

"Okay, okay. Duck for you."

Jake smiled at Kim.

She shook her head.

Jake took the package from Lynn-Lee. "Do you know what he was doing down here?"

"Yeah? Who is he, anyway?"

"He's the Senator's son," Jake said.

Lynn-Lee shook her head.

"What?"

"You go now. Thank you."

"He's dead. Murdered."

Lynn-Lee shook her head. "I don't know anything about a Senator's son and I don't know anything about Jhing Xho. Okay?"

Jake nodded. "Okay."

Lynn-Lee folded her arms over her chest and stared at Jake. "Thanks for the duck."

Jake headed for the front door.

Kim followed. "What are you going to do with that thing?"

"Cook it."

"And who is Jhing Xho?"
"An old friend.

~~~

Wally

Wally stood out at the end of Exit Alley, leaning against the rear wall of their converted warehouse office building with his eyes closed, soaking in the sunshine. Waiting.

He hummed an old, old tune from the 1980s: "With or Without You" by U2.

"Hey, Wally."

"Huh?" He opened his eyes as a patrolman came by on his way to the back parking lot, carrying a shotgun and an equipment bag.

"What are you doing here?"

"Oh, hey, Chris. You know, solving crime and stuff."

"I thought you were working District Four."

"Just a little change of pace. Chasing murderbots now."

"With these guys? And what did you do to deserve that?"

Wally shrugged his shoulders.

"Careful, or you'll never get out." The patrolman headed out to his cruiser.

"You be careful out there."

"Always, man. Always."

Wally closed his eyes again and went back to humming, this time an even older tune, "You Got to Move" by The Rolling Stones.

During the second verse, a second voice joined him. The two finished up singing:

You see that woman
Who walks the street
You see that police
Upon his beat
But then the Lord gets ready
You got to move

"Hey, Sean. Been waiting."

"Yeah. I know."

Wally looked next to him and saw an older man leaning against the building. "How have you been?"

"Let's just get to it, okay?"

"Come on."

They started walking down the back alley together.

"How is Amanda?"

Sean looked at Wally. "You miss her?"

"Sometimes I do."

"I'll tell her, then."

"How's life in the Safety Director's office?" Wally asked.

"Cush job, man. The coffee is never more than an hour old and they have donuts and bagels—and they're always fresh, you know? Melt in your mouth."

"Executive-level crime-fighting."

"Yup, no one throwing angry lead my way. I just push papers from my inbox to my outbox."

"Is your gun still loaded even?"

"You're funny, you know?"

They ducked into a small tavern in the Warehouse District. The room was long, narrow, and darkly lit. It was deserted except for a couple at a back booth.

Motherless Children

"Come on, I'll buy you a drink," Sean said.

"Sure. Why not."

Sean raised his hand to the barmaid. "What do you want?"

"Eh, just a Yuengling for now."

"What…are you trying to impress the boys in Exit Alley? No Maker's Mark?"

"The night is still young, my friend."

"It's two-thirty in the afternoon."

"I told you it was young."

Sean shook his head. "A double shot of Maker's Mark…and a Yuengling for the lightweight here."

"You're a real pal." Wally watched the barmaid serve their drinks. He lifted his pint to Sean.

"Like old times, right?"

"If you say so."

"Yeah. I do."

"So, have you seen the reports?"

Sean sipped and nodded. "The Senator's son?"

"Why me? I was kind of hoping to hide out for a while. Take things nice and slow. You know, chase down a robot or two for giggles."

"The best-laid plans, huh?"

"What does the Safety Commish say?"

"I had to pass it on, you know?"

Wally shook his head.

"You can't bury that stuff. You got any leads?"

"Jake is sniffing around AsiaTown with Kim."

"Kim from Narcotics?"

Wally nodded.

"Keep an eye on her."

"How's that?"

"Nobody else wanted her, so she ended up in the Alley."

"Is she Internal Affairs?" Wally asked.

"Well, I take that back. IA would have taken her, but she said no. Emphatically, so I hear."

"That's a long way to fall, but I guess she didn't hit bottom."

"Not yet, anyway."

Wally sipped his beer. "So, are we going to get some help from downtown?"

"Do you think the Senator's kid is dirty?"

"Too early to tell. But I've got a hunch there's more to this than we know."

"What?"

"Didn't I just say that we don't know?"

Sean downed the rest of his drink in a huge gulp. "Well, then, find out. Fast. Okay? I'll hold him off for a little while."

"Yeah. That'd be great."

"But if the Senator makes a big stink, there's not much I can do about it." Sean stood up. He shrugged his shoulders. "Anyway, I got to get back."

"Thanks, Sean. I appreciate it."

"Keep me up-to-date."

Wally nodded.

"And maybe call Amanda."

"Really?"

Sean called back over his shoulder, "What could it hurt?"

Wally sipped his beer, then realized that Sean left him with the tab.

~~~

The Interview

The Senator sat in Lt. Sands' office, sipping coffee and checking his watch.

Outside, Lt. Sands intercepted Jake and Kim. "No funny business. You've probably got ten minutes."

Jake looked at the Senator. "Ten minutes?"

"If even that."

Jake shook his head. "And not in the interview room?"

Lt. Sands poked Jake in the chest. "Keep it civil. Come on."

Jake motioned Kim to follow the Lieutenant into his office. He whispered into her ear, "Record this on your phone—discreetly."

Kim nodded.

The Senator glanced up and latched his eyes on Kim. He gave her a campaign-certified smile guaranteed to shake a check or a personal favor out of its target. He watched her sit down behind him on the couch.

"Jake here is working your son's case," Lt. Sands said as he sat down at his desk.

Jake watched the Senator watching Kim.

"What happened to those other two fellows you came to the house with?" The Senator looked over at Jake, then back at Kim.

"They're at your son's condo," said Lt. Sands.

"His condo?" The Senator turned to face Lt. Sands.

"It's standard procedure."

"That's not a problem, right?" Jake asked, still standing next to the Senator.

Kim took out her iPhone, hit record, and set it face down on the table beside her.

His smile gone, the Senator shook his head. "No. I suppose not."

"Do you mind if I sit down for a minute?"

The Senator nodded.

"You know we have to ask: is there anyone who might have wanted to harm Mitchell?"

"No. Not that I am aware of."

"What about coming after you?"

"I've thought of that, but I can't think of anyone who would go to those lengths…"

"You do have enemies, though."

"Political adversaries. Certainly. But not killers."

Jake nodded. "Your son was a consultant?"

"Yes. He has an MBA from Wharton. He advises foreign corporations on markets and legislation for doing business in the United States."

"And his father is a Senator."

"Why, yes. That is correct. There is no problem with that, is there?"

"We're just trying to narrow down our investigative focus," said Lt. Sands. He looked at Jake. "We're not drawing any conclusions about that."

"Though it is kind of handy, you being in Congress like that," Jake said.

"There is nothing wrong with helping family."

"What kinds of businesses did he work with?"

"Mostly tech sector. Computers, phones, and such."

"Foreign companies, right?"

"Mostly Asian corporations."

"AsiaTown?" Jake looked back at Kim.

The Senator noticed and looked around her way as well. "What?"

"Mitchell spent a good deal of time there. Do you know what that was about?"

The Senator looked back at Jake. "Maybe he likes Chinese food. Did you think of that?"

"Maybe. But it is where he was killed—or at least where they found his body."

"And you think this is related to his work?"

"I don't know. What do you think?"

"*Jake…*" Lt. Sands said.

"Did he work with any synthoid companies?"

"Honestly, I do not know. He may have. I don't keep track of it."

"Interesting."

The Senator stood up. "I can have my Chief-of-Staff get you that information."

"Thank you, Senator." Lt. Sands stood up as well.

The Senator looked back at Kim and smiled again.

"Oh, are we done here?" Jake asked. "I had a few more questions "

Lt. Sands scowled at Jake.

"And just for your information, I was at a fundraiser that evening. In Pepper Pike."

Jake smiled. "Yes. You, your wife, and your Chief-of-Staff.

We know that already."

"Oh. I see. Very well. I will have that information on my son's clients to you by tomorrow."

Lt. Sands stepped out from behind his desk and escorted the Senator out.

"So, what do you think?" Jake asked Kim.

She shut off her phone. "I think he knows something."

"About AsiaTown?"

"Maybe."

"I don't think it is about Mitchell's work."

'Maybe…"

"I wonder what EC and Wally have found."

~~~

Quay 55

"They don't live like us, do they?" asked Wally. He was standing at the northwest corner windows facing out at the lake and downtown from Mitchell Scofield's apartment in the converted Quay 55 warehouse building on the shoreline.

"You'll drive yourself crazy thinking about it," said EC. He scanned the living room area. "You see an iSlate or a laptop anywhere?"

"What do you think this place goes for? Four or five million?"

EC shook his head. He went over and tried the door to the master bedroom.

Wally turned and looked around at the starkly white modern furniture in the room. "White? How does he keep it so clean? Who lives like this?"

"Are you going to help, or what?" EC went into the master bedroom.

Wally shrugged. He wandered around the living room, wiping his latex-gloved hand on the tabletops and noticing no dust at all. "I don't see any wall warts out here."

"Nothing in here," EC came back out. "What about the other bedrooms upfront?"

Wally went into the bedroom on the right. "Yeah, this one looks like an office."

EC wandered through the other bedroom and joined Wally. "Nothing in the other one. Just a guest room. What about here?"

Wally stood by the window staring out across Burke Lakefront airport at the Brown's First Energy stadium. "Look! A dust spot. So, he probably had one in here."

"You are going to drive yourself crazy," EC said, as he started searching through the drawers on Mitchell's desk.

A key slid into the front door and turned the lock.

Wally looked at EC. He moved to the bedroom door.

EC drew his pistol as the door opened and shut.

"Mitchell, where the hell are you?" High heels clicked down the front entryway, heading towards the master bedroom.

Wally stepped out of the front office. He saw a blonde head of hair disappear inside. He took a couple of steps forward and waited.

"Damn it," came out of the bedroom. The high heels came back Wally's way. They stopped in the doorway. "Huh?"

Wally smiled as he took in the twenty-something woman, from her stilettos, up her perfectly tanned legs, low-cut dress, and straight blonde hair that curled just beneath her shoulders.

"Who the hell are you?" she asked taking off her sunglasses.

Wally pulled the left side of his jacket aside to show the detective's badge clipped to his belt. "I'm Wally. And you would be…"

"Where's Mitchell?"

EC stepped out behind Wally. He held his Glock with both hands, pointing it down and away from the woman.

"And that's my partner, EC." Wally smiled. "You made him nervous."

"Where is Mitchell?" she asked, again.

"Well, he is kind of dead," Wally said. "And you would be…who?"

She walked over to the kitchen counter and sat herself down on a barstool. She slowly crossed her legs. "Dead?"

Wally stepped around to the other side of the counter. He nodded. "Hey, come on. You know we have to ask this stuff."

EC lowered his gun to his side but kept it out.

"Did you see any women's clothes in the master?" Wally asked EC.

"No. Nothing," EC answered.

"But you have a key," Wally said. "Girlfriend? Fiancé? Or maybe something a bit more…*casual?*"

"How did he die?"

Wally looked over at EC. He shook his head. "You do know that we're the police, right? You saw my badge and everything. We're the ones who get to ask the questions."

"Yes. Right. I am Monique and I have…an arrangement."

Wally smiled. "Now, that's better. What kind of arrangement? Work? Play? Or otherwise?"

"Hmmm. I would say, yes."

EC slid his pistol into his holster. "And where were you last night?"

"Hong Kong. Is that when he was killed?"

"Yes, it was."

Monique leaned down over the counter and rested her head in her hands. She shook her head slowly.

"And what would you know about that?"

"About what? His death? Nothing. Nothing at all." Monique glanced up at Wally. "You do know who Mitchell Scofield is, right?"

Wally gave Monique a dumb look. He shrugged at EC and shook his head. "We're cops. We kind of know what we're doing."

"The son of Senator Scofield," EC said. "It still doesn't answer who you are, why you have a key, and why you are here."

"Well, we do work together."

"And is that why you were in Hong Kong?" Wally asked.

"Yes. Yes, it is."

"And what was that about?" asked EC.

"I'd rather not say. It was confidential."

"Confidential doesn't really work in this instance. You know, murder and stuff."

"Murder?" she asked.

"It was, indeed," Wally said.

"I was meeting with a client. And, no, he did not kill Mitchell, either. Remember *Hong Kong?* So I don't know why I have to get into it with you."

Wally shook his head again. "Maybe you should come downtown with us for a little bit."

"Are you detaining me?"

"Well…you could be a material witness."

"I think I told you, I was in Hong Kong."

"Uh…"

"If you are detaining me, then *Waaally,* I would have to have my lawyer present—from Stein, Baylor, and Stein—before I would even consider answering any of your questions. And I think he would quite politely advise me to—you know—keep my trap shut. Do you have that kind of time to waste?"

Wally looked at EC.

He shook his head.

"Well, I guess not."

"Yeah, I didn't think so."

"Let me see some ID," EC asked.

"Certainly, *officer.*" She pulled her driver's license from the pocket on the back of her phone and handed it over.

"Monique De la Croix…" EC took a picture of her license with his phone. He held it up, then handed it back. "Look here, Wally. She's from Washington DC."

"Do you know Senator Scofield?" Wally asked.

"I just might—and maybe a few others, too." Monique smiled seductively. "Alrighty, then. I think I'll be on my way."

"Where are you staying?" EC asked. "In case we have more questions."

"Well, certainly not here," Monique said. "The Marriott downtown, I suppose."

Wally sighed.

"Are we done here?" Monique asked.

Wally and EC looked at one another and shrugged.

"Good, then." Monique headed towards the door. "You gentlemen have a good day, alright?"

They watched her leave the apartment.

"I'm not sure what happened here," Wally said.

"Yeah. Me neither," said EC.

~~~

Little Italy

He got his usual table at Momma Santas and ordered the veal parmesan again. He was alone.

Outside, it waited.

He sipped his Chianti and carefully scanned the Friday night crowd. Every table was full and the dining room percolated with the happy cacophony of eating, drinking, and T.G.I.F release.

He discreetly scanned his fellow diners. A loud group of teenagers shoveled down pizza. A pair of thirty-something suburban couples laughed loudly and refilled their wine glasses, yet again. In the back, an older couple ate quietly, staring down at their plates. A young mother and father fussed over their two young children, trying to keep them occupied while they waited for their food. The father leaned over to gently scold the wired-up boy. The mother affectionately rubbed his older sister's shoulder and asked what the fifth-grader was drawing on the back of her placemat. He stared a bit too long and allowed a crooked smile to scar his large jowly face.

Barbara brought him back to his own table serving his veal parmesan. "Here you go, Mr. Eliot."

"Oh, yes. Excellent." He looked down at the plate and took a deep breath. Shaking out his napkin, Mr. Eliot carefully tucked a corner behind his neatly knotted tie and spread the sides to cover the large spread of his abdomen. "It looks quite delicious."

Barbara looked over at the two young children, then back again. "Can I get you anything else?"

He looked up at her and gave a little grin. "Perhaps some more wine? Please?"

She reached for the decanter and refilled his wine glass.

Mr. Eliot enjoyed being served.

"Anything else?"

"Thank you. No." He grabbed his knife and fork European-style and cut into the veal. He took a bite. "Mmm…delicious."

When she was gone, Mr. Eliot gazed back at the children one last time, then he turned his full attention to his plate. He slowly savored his meal, taking extra care not to splatter spaghetti sauce on his five-thousand-dollar suit.

He finished his wine and left Barbara a generous cash tip.

"How was everything?" the hostess asked, running his credit card.

"*Eccellente,* my dear. As always." He checked himself again for splatter. He scowled a bit at the tiny red splotches on his shirt, then collected his card and receipt. He smiled. "It's a write-off."

The night air was cool. Mr. Eliot looked across the street at Corbo's bakery. He saw his rotund reflection in the store window. He smiled at himself. He had a certain…stature. Seeing through himself into the storefront, he decided, *Oh, why not?*

He crossed Mayfield Boulevard and went in for a pair of cannoli.

From just down East 123rd Street, the synthoid IDed Mr. Eliot via facial recognition—though his girth was not a dead giveaway—and observed him purchase his pastries and leave the bakery, heading down the hill towards Euclid Avenue. It followed on the opposite side of the street. The very large heat signature from his girth made for a particularly easy target.

The synthoid was lost in the shuffle, dressed in khakis and a golf shirt. Its facial features were modeled after a young Kevin Costner: blonde and bland and generally ignored on the street.

It wove effortlessly through the flow of people coming up the hill, quickly closing the gap as it followed Mr. Eliot to his BMW parked in the Rapid Transit station lot at the far end of Little Italy.

Mr. Eliot shifted the cannoli to his other hand to retrieve his key fob from his jacket pocket.

It closed the thirty-foot gap between them in just a couple of silent seconds. The synthoid reached around his neck and latched onto Mr. Eliot's throat, closing its hydraulic grip to choke off his airway and gag his voice. Without effort, it lifted him off his feet.

Mr. Eliot's legs began to flail. He dropped his keys and then finally his cannoli. He grabbed helplessly at the hand around his neck. He tried to gag, but could not.

It just squeezed harder until Mr. Eliot's feet began swinging less and less until they hung limply down. His eyes rolled back, flecked with petechial hemorrhaging. The synthoid held him there until it felt the pulse throb of the carotid artery cease against the sensors under its Dermaloy skin.

The synthoid lowered its arm and effortlessly dragged Mr. Eliot like a lifeless doll down across the rapid transit tracks to the CSX freight train rails and tossed him face down.

Pulling Mr. Eliot's shirt out of the back of his pants, the synthoid activated the laser behind the right eye socket and burned a barcode into the small of his back

It photographed the code. It turned Mr. Eliot over and took a picture of his flaccid face, then uploaded the files to a private cloud server directory through the Atlas Grid.

The synthoid walked up the CSX rails and disappeared into the night.

Mr. Eliot would not be missed until Monday when he failed to appear for his client's bail hearing.

Mining

Exit Alley was empty and dark. The human cleaning crew had moved through the area, sweeping the rugs and wiping down all the file cabinets, tables and desks—except for Jake's cluttered cubicle which had a "Do Not Disturb, No Moleste, Ne Pas Déranger, просьба не беспокоить, 邪魔しないでください " hotel door sign prominently displayed

Q sat in the murder room at the conference table. The overhead lights were dimmed. His face glowed from the displays of his laptops—the police issued unit given to him by EC and his personal MacBook Pro, which he VPNed into the Atlas Grid through the Department's iNode. It gave him the unfettered access he needed to search and privacy from the clowns in IT.

The police laptop had several windows open. The numbers scrolled across the screen as macros ran to compare the victims' twelve-digit barcodes against different databases for matches. Q felt it was a futile effort, but it showed him actually "working" on the case.

Meanwhile, with his MacBook, Q used law enforcement's less restricted access to search the digital ledgers of cryptocurrency mining sites, searching for the missing four hundred and fifty million dollars hijacked from Stein, Baylor & Stein while Jake and Q were hunting for the Baron.

By the time the lawyers finally got him the private key, the money had been moved out of their client's account. Using Block Explorers, he quickly found the account where the money ended up and quietly watched. The four hundred and fifty million dollars sat there untouched for several months. Q figured when the Baron was killed it would be forever locked up in the blockchain, so he set up a mining site and discreetly began a Birthday Attack on the account to crack the hash code.

Then, the Bitcoins suddenly disappeared. Thank God for the Barcode Murders and his consulting contract with Lt. Sands.

With his MacBook, Q searched for several hours until he was finally able to identify a number of "Atomic Swaps" where the Bitcoins had been broken down into ninety million dollar chunks and moved through different Ethereum, Ripple, Litecoin, and Bitcoin blockchains accounts until it was reassembled at a Cayman Island-based crypto exchange.

"You are sly, but so am I," Q whispered to himself, as he attached a sniffer algorithm to the transactions and set up his own account and node in the exchange.

But if the Baron is dead…then who is working the account?

~~~

Jhing Xho

Kim and Jake sat in a Starbucks on Clifton Boulevard waiting.

"And what are we doing here?" Kim asked as she sipped from a *Grande* Dark Roast.

"Waiting."

"Duh…"

"How can you drink that stuff?" Jake asked.

"What are you, a wimp?"

"I thought you guys liked tea."

"Oh, so now who's being politically in-correct?"

"He likes the place. I don't know why, but he does."

"And why do you want me here, if he's your old friend?" Kim asked.

"Your Mandarin is better than mine, okay?"

Kim sighed and shook her head.

"Mmm…You know these are delicious." A Chinese man, mid-forties with his hair slicked back and dressed neatly in a suit and tie, sat down at their table.

"What is that you are drinking?" Jake asked.

"A Caramel Ribbon Crunch Crème Frappuccino." Jhing Xho took a large slurp out of his straw. He held the cup out towards Jake. "Would you like to try it?"

Jake leaned back and away. "Thank you, no."

"And you would be…" Jhing Xho asked Kim.

"She would be my new partner, Kim," said Jake.

Jhing Xho looked Kim over and slowly nodded his head. "Uh-huh, uh-huh. Very nice."

"Hey!" Kim said.

Jhing Xho looked at Jake and asked, *That* Kim?"

Jake shrugged.

Kim crossed her arms against her chest and glared at Jhing Xho.

"And speaking of which, how is Maddie?"

"We weren't—but she's doing just fine."

"In Washington, DC, I understand? That is such a long, long way away, no?" Jhing Xho looked at Kim and winked.

Kim hid her scowl behind her dark roast.

Jhing Xho and Kim talked in Chinese for a few moments. Jake followed along.

Kim smiled at Jake and asked, "Did you get that?"

"He says that to all the girls he meets," Jake said.

Jhing Xho smiled at Kim. He slowly drew a long, sucking drink through his straw.

"Well, I think he's right." Kim smiled back at Jhing Xho. *"Xièxiè."*

Jhing Xho nodded slightly towards her.

Jake shook his head.

"And you have some questions for me about Mitchell Scofield, do you not?" Jhing Xho asked.

"He seemed to be playing in your sandbox."

Jhing Xho took another long sip of Caramel Ribbon Crunch Crème Frappuccino, then set the cup down. "Of course, I knew of him. How could you not? His father is a United States Senator."

"And what was he up to?" Jake asked.

Motherless Children

"Ah, yes. What can I say?" Jhing Xho looked at Kim and smiled. "Not everyone favors gorgeous young women…you know, like we do, my friend."

"Mitchell?" she asked.

Jhing Xho shrugged.

"So what?" Jake asked.

"He works as an importer/exporter, doesn't he?"

"His father told us he helps overseas companies do business here in the United States," said Kim.

"Yes. Yes, indeed. And what do these overseas companies do?"

"Mostly electronics, I guess. High tech."

"And where do you work now, Jake?"

"Artificial Crimes Unit.".

Jhing Xho nodded. "And this work involves…*high technology*…does it not?"

Jake nodded.

"Some people say with these things, these synthoids, we are calling upon demons."

"I don't make a moral judgment on them. I just chase them down when somebody hacks them to cross the line," Jake said.

"And where is that line, Jake?"

"Murder, for one."

"Like Mitchell?"

"Like Mitchell. Yes," said Jake.

"Indeed. How unfortunate for him. But why do you suppose that was?"

"I don't know." Jake shook his head.

"And there are others, too. Am I right?"

Jake and Kim both nodded.

"No connections between them, though—as far as you know."

"They were…" Jake looked at Kim. "…marked."

"Yes. The tattoos. Barcodes—am I right?"

Jake sat back. "You know?"

"How did you find out?" Kim asked.

Jhing Xho took a drink of his Frappuccino. "It is of little matter, really."

"What do they mean?"

"Of that, I do not know. Something I am sure." Jhing Xho gazed out the front window, then back at Jake. "Are there other lines that one can cross?"

"Isn't murder enough?"

"Oh, I do not know. *Dāng yīgè zhìzhě zhixiàng yuèqiú shí, mángrén huì jianchá shouzhi.*"

"When a wise man points at the moon the imbecile examines the finger," Kim said. "Confucius."

"An *imbecile?*" Jake asked.

"Of course, not you, my friend. See the moon. But not everyone sees it…or wants to. There are other things that cross lines besides murder. Mr. Scofield never hurt anyone…specifically, I suppose. But certainly, what he did was…*unsavory.*" Jhing Xho smiled. "Not that I am one to judge. It is your rules, which he does not obey. Not mine."

"Which rules are those?"

"They are of little matter to me, you see. It is not of my doing. So, I have no interest." Jhing Xho stood up. "But you should know that it is the motherless children…They are the ones now being protected."

Jake sat back and regarded Jhing Xho. *'Okay…"*

"You must be careful, Jake. There is a war going on. Maybe no one is right, but certainly some are wrong. And some of those people are very powerful."

"Like the Senator?" Jake asked.

Jhing Xho smiled. Then, he turned and walked away, sipping his Frappuccino.

His bodyguards seated by the entrance stood. One held the door open and he followed the other one out.

Moonglow

Wally sat alone in the unmarked Crown Vic cruiser parked on Madison Avenue in Lakewood. He stared at the storefront across the street, a witchcraft store called Moonglow.

Foot traffic was light for a Saturday afternoon, but he still sat and watched the front door for another half an hour. No one went in or left the store. Finally, he got out to cross in the middle of the block and push in through an old wooden door. A bell on the door rang.

The store was comfortably dim, but not dark. He took a deep breath and smiled. He always liked the smell of incense. Wally noticed glitter spread all over the floor.

There were no other customers inside, so Wally wandered about, taking in the trinkets, crystals, jewelry, statuettes, plaques, paintings, photos, books, cards, and coffee mugs, all artfully arranged on regular furniture—end tables, dressers, and coffee tables. The pieces skewed towards empty trees, crescent moons, five-pointed stars, and odd gnome heads. There were a few racks of scarves, hats, and T-shirts screen printed with Wicca and witchcraft icons. Wally pawed through a canvas rack of ready-to-frame photos. A dilute calico cat appeared out of nowhere to lean against his shins.

"Well, well. As I live and breathe," said a low female voice behind him. "And don't you kick Artemis."

"You don't happen to have any cute cat pictures, do you?" Wally asked without turning around. He continued to flip through the prints. "You know, ones I can hang on my office wall for inspiration—like 'Hang in There' or 'Never Give Up' or 'How Do You Work a Can Opener?' Uplifting stuff like that. To keep me motivated."

Before he knew it, Amanda ran over, leapt on his back, and wrapped her arms around his neck. She whispered in his ear, "You are a jerk."

"Yeah. I know. They keep telling me that at work."

She nibbled on his ear lobe.

"Hey, that tickles."

Amanda hopped down, turned Wally around, and gave him a big hug. She was half a foot shorter than him.

He leaned down and smelled her long, dark, curly hair. A platinum blonde streak ran down the right side of her head.

"Come on." She took his hand, led him to a round oak table at the back of the shop, and sat him down. "You want some tea?"

Wally shook his head.

"Or water, maybe?"

"Yeah. That's good."

She went in back and brought out a bottled water.

"Thanks." Wally unscrewed the top and took a drink. "What's with the glitter, anyway?"

"It attracts fairies."

"Oh…okay." He smiled.

Amanda smiled back. "It's really great to see you again."

"Uh-huh…so, how are things going?"

"Good—really good. I mean, it doesn't look like it right now, but..." She sat down next to Wally and gently rubbed his leg.

Wally nodded and scanned around the empty shop.

"No, really. I'm fine."

Wally looked at her with a goofy grin. "Good. I'm glad."

"And what brings you down here into my wicked, wicked lair?"

Wally took another drink of water. "Well, I talked to your dad the other day."

"Uh-huh."

"He said to call, but I thought maybe I'd stop by instead."

"And how's he doing in his big important job downtown in the Commissioner's office?"

"I think he likes it. Lots of fresh pastry and stuff."

"He needs to cut back, you know?"

Wally nodded. "Yeah, don't we all."

Amanda rubbed his belly. "I think it's cute on you."

"I've been working on my massive middle body strength, you know."

"And how's your mom?"

"If someone doesn't give her a grandchild soon, she's going to go totally postal."

"You?"

Wally shook his head. "I got nothing."

"Maybe I could work up a little potion for you."

"That's not really what I need."

"Oh yeah? And what would *that* be...exactly?"

"The love of a good woman would be a start."

She smiled at Wally and stroked his cheek.

"Anyway, can you mix one up to make bad karma go away?"

"Aw, what's wrong, Wally?"

"Oh, it's just this stupid case I'm working on now. I just know there's going to be big trouble."

"Why's that?"

"You know Senator Scofield?"

Amanda shook her head. "Come on. It's me. I don't care about that crap. What's he done?"

"Well, his son got killed."

"Got killed?"

"Was murdered."

"Mmmm…" Amanda nodded her head.

"And there are two others."

"That doesn't sound good."

"No. It isn't." Wally leaned forward and put his elbows to his knees.

"Is that the bad karma?"

He shook his head. "We went to the Senator's mansion in Bratenahl the day after—me and my partner, EC, and my Lieutenant—to tell him and his wife. I watched him closely. Very closely. There was something…lost about his eyes. Like they were black and empty inside."

"Wally, he's a politician. What did you expect?"

"Nothing. He just sat there at his desk shuffling papers around. He didn't even reach out to his wife."

"They are just not real people—like you and me. Everything is a big show for them. They are always under the spotlight. People are always looking and waiting for them to screw up—which they usually do."

Wally shook his head slightly. "He wasn't hiding anything. They were empty. Like a reptile."

"I don't have a potion to cure that."

"Yeah, I didn't think so."

The front door jingled with the little bell as three women came into the shop.

Wally stood up. "I should go."

"No, stay."

"Maybe lunch or dinner or something…"

Amanda stood up and gave Wally a hug. "Sorry I couldn't help out."

"You're right. He's a politician. What can you do?" Wally headed towards the door.

"Call me."

Wally waved back over his shoulder and left.

~~~

The CSX Track Line

"Chesapeake and Ohio Railway and the Seaboard Coast Line," said EC.

"Huh?" Wally asked.

"CSX. That's what it is. These are their lines."

The sunrise glinted off the tracks.

"And you would know this how?"

"Stupid kid stuff. I liked trains."

Wally nodded.

They stood leaning against the front fender of a Crown Vic, sipping coffee out of to-go cups and watching CSI techs take their initial crime scene photographs.

"He's, ah, kind of a lard-ass, you think?" Wally asked, looking at the rotund body of Mr. Eliot sprawled on the other side of the railroad tracks.

EC sighed.

"Well, that's Woodrow's problem," Jake said, referring to the coroner, as he and Kim walked up to the cruiser. "I hope he brings some boys with muscles."

"The patrol guys called it in." EC pointed to a group of uniformed officers standing around their radio cars. "Seems like a commuter on the Rapid reported it."

"Barcode?" Kim asked.

"Price check on aisle five," Wally said.

"Who is he?" Jake asked.

A bunny suit boy waved the detectives into the crime scene.

"I don't know. Let's go find out," said EC, pulling on latex gloves.

Wally held up the yellow crime scene tape for the others, then followed them in.

"He's a boatload," said the CSI tech as they got to the body.

"What do you think?" Wally asked. "Four? Four-fifty?"

"Three and a quarter, at least," said the CSI tech.

"I'll be able to tell you more when I get him on the table," Woody said as he came up behind them.

"Hey, Elvis," Jake said to Woody. "What's shaking?"

EC squatted next to the body and searched his pants pockets.

"Huh. I know you. You. And you." Woody stood next to Jake and pointed at him, EC, then Wally. He pointed at Kim. "But who would you be, *darlin'*?"

"My new partner," said Jake.

"Kim." She put her hands on her hips and leaned back away from the coroner.

"Uh-huh. Well, I am very glad to meet you," Woody said with a toothy grin. "You are welcome in my morgue anytime—with or without Jake. Now, if you'll excuse me, I have to try to find this guy's liver."

"Anthony Eliot," EC said, pulling a driver's license out of a wallet.

"Really? Fat Tony?" Wally said.

"You know this guy, too?" EC asked.

"Well, not personally. Criminal defense attorney. Some say he's mobbed up, but me, personally, I don't know. You'd have to ask Organized Crime."

"I doubt that has anything to do with the barcodes." Jake stepped up and started walking around the body examining it from all angles.

"This guy's been toast for a while," Woody said, pulling a temperature probe out of the body. "I'd say probably Friday night sometime."

"Where's the tattoo?" Jake asked.

"Lower back. Down here." Woody pulled up Mr. Eliot's shirt and pointed.

Jake stooped down to look.

"Do you know what they mean?" Woody asked.

"Q's working on it." He took out his phone and snapped a picture. "Get your guys over here and roll him over."

Woody waved to his technicians, who carried a stretcher over the rocks to the body. "Let's take a look at Mister Fat Tony, why don't we."

The technicians took three times to roll Mr. Eliot on his back.

Woody pulled back the eyelids. "Yup. Petechial hemorrhaging. No doubt he was strangled, too."

"Just like the others," said Kim.

"Yeah, you can feel it, too." Woody probed around Mr. Eliot's throat.

Jake pulled on gloves and knelt down beside Woody. He turned Mr. Eliot's head left then right. He looked carefully at his left hand, then his right. He took a picture of his face.

"You know, that's a five thousand dollar suit," Woody whispered to Jake. "Not bad, eh?"

Jake lifted the collars of the suit coat. He pointed at tiny red splotches on the shirt. "What do you think?"

Woody leaned over, putting his eyes an inch above the shirt.

"Well, normally I'd like to do some testing. But I think it's marinara sauce."

Jake turned his head up the hill towards Little Italy. "Thanks, doc. We've got a clue."

"That will cost you a dollar," Woody said.

"Put it on my tab." Jake stood up and pulled off his gloves. "I think we're done."

"Okay. Bag his hands and get him in the van," Woody said to his techs. "See you downtown?"

Jake nodded. He turned to Kim. "So, what do you think about *Italiano* food?"

"This early in the morning?" Kim asked.

"We can get some donuts from one of the bakeries."

"I need more coffee."

"Come on."

They headed towards the crime scene tape.

"Hey, Jake," Wally said. "Patrol thinks they found his car in the Rapid lot. There's a key fob and some smashed-up cannoli."

"See, I told you. Donuts," Jake said to Kim.

They followed Wally over to the black BMW. EC was in the passenger seat digging through the glove compartment.

"It's his Beemer," said EC. "Nothing out of the ordinary inside. He probably got taken before he got in."

Jake knelt down by the stepped-on Corbo's Bakery bag.

"You are not going to say it, are you?" Wally asked.

Jake looked up at him and smiled.

"Say what?" asked Kim.

"Classic movie quotes," EC said wearily. "Don't get them started."

"Just have CSI get a picture of the footprint," Jake said. "I'm thinking it belongs to the synthoid. Tony was fat, but his feet were pretty small."

"Man, that's a long haul for four bills," Wally said looking back towards where the body was found.

"Synthoids are like fricking ants," EC said. "They can lift fifty times their own weight."

"Come on. Let's go get you some joe," Jake said to Kim. They headed down to the street and started walking up Murray Hill.

"Fifty times?"

"Do I look like Wikipedia? EC knows all that technical stuff."

They crossed Mayfield Road and went into Corbo's Bakery.

"*Officers*…what can I get you?" asked the man dressed in baker's whites behind the counter.

"I think we need some coffee," Jake said.

"We can do." He poured two cups and handed them over the counter. "On me."

Before Jake could say anything, Kim put a ten-dollar bill down on the counter. "Thanks. Keep the change."

"Oh, yeah…" Jake looked at her and nodded.

"Just keeping it all above board," she said.

"Right."

"Do you know this guy?" Kim pointed her phone at the baker with Mr. Eliot's driver's license on it.

He shrugged. "We get a lot of people in here."

"Come on," Jake said.

"Look. I don't want any trouble. Okay?"

"He's dead. Is that going to cause any trouble?"

"Dead?" the baker asked.

"With two of your cannoli right next to his body."

The baker shook his head. "Fat Tony. Every Friday night. Veal Parmiagan across the street at Mama Santas and two cannoli to go."

"By himself?" Kim asked.

The baker nodded.

"Every Friday?" Jake asked.

"Every Friday. All by himself. I don't know anything else. I don't know where he goes. I don't know what he does—and I don't want to, okay?"

"Give me some cannoli." Jake asked Kim, "Do you want something?"

"No. Thanks."

Jake put a twenty-dollar bill down on the counter. He looked at Kim. "This goes against my nature."

She shook her head.

"Keep the change." Jake grabbed the pastry bag.

"So, what's that mean?" Kim asked as they left.

"That Fat Tony was still hungry."

~~~

Roadkill

His city-marked pickup truck turned down Erieside Avenue. He drove past the Browns football stadium, the Science Center, and the Rock & Roll Hall of Fame. He crossed East Ninth Street onto North Marginal Drive and followed alongside the runways at Burke Lakefront Airport. Just east of the airport property, he slowed to a stop and hit his flashers.

He hopped out of the truck, dressed in a hard hat, safety glasses, and a bright yellow vest. He pulled on thick leather gloves, then grabbed a shovel and rake from the back of the truck. In the middle of the lane ahead, he scooped the dead raccoon onto the shovel, dumping it into the truck bed followed by the shovel and rake.

He leaned on the back gate and looked over at the Quay 55 apartment building where Mitchell Scofield lived.

He smirked, then went on his way.

He crossed I-90 on East 55th Street and came back down Lakeside Road through the Warehouse District, then out the Shoreway to the statue of Richard Wagner in Edgewater Park.

He came back over the Cuyahoga River on the Detroit-Superior Bridge and followed Superior Avenue into AsiaTown.

He drove east on Chester Avenue, cut up to Murray Hill, and parked across from the Rapid Station parking lot to watch the police work Mr. Eliot's crime scene.

~~~

5 Alive News

When Kim and Jake got back to their cruiser, a young woman dressed in a dark, short-skirted, pinstriped business suit and heavily made-up leaned against the front quarter panel. Her shoulder-length blonde hair was locked in place with Paul Mitchell Firm Style Freeze & Shine Super Spray Hairspray.

"Well, hey there, Jake. What do you know?" Her voice was cool, clear, and a bit husky. It cut right into his spine.

Jake lowered his head and shook it.

"Hey, I know you, too," the woman said, pointing at Kim. "You used to be in Narcotics, right? And, well…had some issues with Internal Affairs, I understand. Is that why you're hanging out with Jake and the geeks?"

"And you would be?" Kim asked impatiently.

"Kristie."

"From Channel Five news," Jake finished.

Kristie reached out to shake Kim's hand. "Is he in one of his grumpy moods?"

Kim bared her teeth. She squeezed back a bit hard. "Don't really know…It's kind of hard to tell."

"What can we do for you, Kristie?" Jake asked.

She ignored him and leaned into Kim. "You know about his last partner, Maddie, right? There was a certain…*involvement*…" Kristie looked over at Jake. "Isn't that right?"

"Him? And me?" Kim sneered at Jake. "Yeah, I don't think so."

"And how is Maddie doing down in DC with the FBI, Jake? And the little guy, too? What's his name? Wyatt?"

"*No comment,*" Jake said.

"On Maddie or the case?"

"Both."

"Gee, he is in a grumpy mood," Kristie said to Kim. "And that's too bad. I thought maybe we could mix business with pleasure, you know?" She winked at Jake.

"With him?" Kim asked.

"He's actually quite an *interesting* fellow." Kristie smiled at Jake. "Anyway, this is number four, right? Sounds a bit like another serial killer thing going on here."

Jake gave Kristie a half-smile. "Come on, you know we can't discuss—"

"Oh, of course, I know all that. But if we were pals…" Kristie rubbed Jake's arm. "Real pals…"

"We could be, but…"

"You still have my number, right?"

Jake nodded.

"Good." Kristie pointed at her cameraman standing with his hands on his hips behind the tripod aimed with a view of the tracks. "I think he's ready for me."

"Off you go, then," Jake said.

"We'll be in touch—*soon.*" Kristie smiled at Kim. "Try to keep him out of trouble, okay? Maddie didn't do such good a job."

Kim and Jake watched her saunter over and take her place in front of the camera.

"You…*and her?*" Kim asked.

Motherless Children

"Life gets complicated sometimes."
"Yeah, not that complicated."

~~~

The Murder Board

Jake sat at the far end of the table in the Exit Alley conference room burning holes in the murder board with his eyes.

Kim stood up close, slowly stepping from left to right, examining the bodies of the victims at the crime scenes, yet again. "I don't see anything."

"It's there...somewhere." Jake sipped his coffee.

Lt. Sands came in and sat next to Jake with a to-go cup of coffee. He looked at the murder board, then back at Jake. "Well?"

"You want a cannoli?" Jake pushed the Corbo's bag over in front of Lt. Sands.

"Is this all you've got? Four dead bodies and a bag of pastries?"

"It's a marathon, not a sprint."

"Give me one of those." Lt. Sands grabbed the bag. "Captain Caldwell has got my number on speed dial. I've got to give him something for the Safety Director."

"Working on it, boss," said Jake.

"What about Q? What's he come up with on the barcodes."

Kim looked at Jake. "Well?"

"Nothing in the GTIN databases. Don't seem to be regular bank account numbers."

"Serial numbers?" Kim asked.

"Could be...but to what?"

Lt. Sands closed his eyes and took another bite of cannoli.

EC and Wally came in.

Wally set down a banker's box on the table. "You'll never guess what we found at Fat Tony's office."

"What's that?" Lt. Sands asked around a mouthful of cannoli.

"Mr. Burr and Mr. Whistler seem to have been clients of Fat Tony," said EC.

"They gave you the files?" Kim asked.

"Oh, they moaned and complained," said EC, "but it's nice having some muscle on your side."

Wally flexed his biceps with his fists over his shoulders like Hulk Hogan.

"And?" Jake asked.

"Looks like Burr got caught trolling for a freshman at St. Joseph's. And Whistler seems to have had an affair with a underaged girl. He said she was a waitress that lied on her job application. Yeah…right."

"What about the Senator's son? Anything there?" Lt. Sands asked.

"Didn't see his name in the client files," Wally said. "But three out of four ain't bad."

"That's not what the Safety Director wants to hear," said Lt. Sands. "He doesn't care about Burr and Whistler."

"Hey, are those from Little Italy?" Wally pointed at the Corbo's bag.

"Knock yourself out," Jake said.

Wally popped half a cannoli into his mouth.

Kim went over to the banker's box and started flipping through files. "Can we use this stuff? I mean, with attorney-client privilege?"

"You want the info or not?" EC asked.

"I don't want to know about any of that." Lt. Sands stood up and pointed at the boxes. He sighed, heading towards the door. "Just get me something. And quick."

EC opened his iSlate. "I don't know why this didn't show up in the initial background checks."

"I love these things." Wally shoved the other half of the cannoli in his mouth and reached into the bag. He looked at Jake. "We good?"

"Knock yourself out."

"Well, that's why Fat Tony is so good at lawyering," Wally said. "Those mob guys demand the best. Just make it all go away."

"But Sands is right. Where does Mitchell fit into all of this?" Jake asked. "And nothing at his apartment?"

"Just Monique De la Croix…You'd like her." Wally sighed. "But we checked with the airlines and she was in Hong Kong the night Mitchell was killed."

"Did you check her passport with the State Department?" Jake asked.

"Not yet," said EC.

"I'd like to know where else she's been hanging out," said Jake.

"You know, there are a few other files in here with Burr and Whistler," said Kim.

"Give me a name," said EC.

"Try this one: Stanislaw, Dante." She spelled the last name.

EC typed. He waited. "Nothing."

"He was arrested three years ago for solicitation. He got caught up in a vice sting."

EC shrugged his shoulders.

"How about, Robert Bennington?"

EC typed. "There are three."

"He lives in Battery Park."

"Nope…Nope…Nope."

"How many names?" Jake asked.

"Looks like a half-dozen."

"Maybe you guys should chase those other guys down tomorrow," Jake said to EC and Wally.

"Will do," said Wally. He stood up and yawned. "I'm heading home."

"Yeah, me, too." EC snapped his iSlate shut. "We'll catch up tomorrow."

EC and Wally left.

"Hey, what are the docket numbers for Burr and Whistler?" Jake asked. "Do they match the barcodes?"

Kim shuffled through the files. "They don't match."

"There's got to be something there on this angle with the women and prostitutes."

"But there's nothing sexual in the murders."

"I think it's payback."

"Payback for what?" asked Kim. "And why the robots?"

"I don't know." Jake leaned back in his chair and looked back at the murder board. "It's in there…somewhere."

"You staying?" Kim asked.

"Yeah. For a bit."

"Okay. I'm clocking out."

Jake nodded, staring at the murder board.

~~~

Maddie

It was after midnight when Jake got back to his apartment. As soon as he lay down on the couch and put his feet up on the arm, his phone rang. He dug it out of his pocket. Maddie.

"Hey," he answered. "Is everything okay?"

"Yeah. You were up, right?"

"Been kind of a long day."

"Mmmm…"

Jake just listened.

"Are, ah, are you working the Scofield case?"

"Why? What does the Senator want?"

"I'm not sure. But some guy from the seventh floor came down and talked to my SSA about it."

"So, the Director's involved?"

"I'm guessing the Senator reached out to him."

"Closed-door meeting?"

"Yeah—at first. Then they asked me into the conference room."

"And…"

"They asked me about you."

Jake sat up on the couch. "And what did they want to know?"

"They wanted to know if you would be able to solve the case."

"Local yokel kind of thing."

Maddie sighed. "Something like that."

"Yeah, and what did you say?"

"Don't be mean. I told them that one way or another you would get to the bottom of it." Maddie paused. "And are you?"

"You know this is part of a serial crime, right?"

"They didn't say that."

"Well, right now we've got two other victims—I mean three, after today."

"All Munchausened?"

"Seems so. They were all tattooed with barcodes. Did they say anything about that?"

"No."

"That's between you and me. Q's checking into it."

"He's back?"

"Consulting agreement."

"Who are the other guys?" Maddie asked.

"Well, the guy today was a mob lawyer named Anthony Eliot, who, it just so happens, represented two of the other guys on sex crime charges."

"What about Mitchell?"

"No connection—*yet.*"

"The mob, huh?" Maddie asked.

"Do you think the Senator's trying to cut us off at the pass? That seems kind of lame."

"I don't know."

"So, what did the Senator's son really do for a living?" Jake smiled. He could imagine her frowning at the other end of the line. "Come on, I know you checked."

"Hard to tell. He's some kind of import/export consultant—I guess more of an importer, though. I checked his website, A.V. Meridian, but it just seems to be a lot of word salad mumbo-jumbo."

"Yeah, that's what we got, too. Any federal paperwork on

him? He had to have something with the State Department, right? Or Commerce?" Jake rubbed his eyes. "And, hey, why were they talking to the Artificial Crimes group there? Because of you? Or something else?

"Yeah, I don't know. Probably just me. You and I are not a big secret around here."

"What are you working on?"

"Still just the usual terrorism stuff."

"I don't think that's what Mitchell was up to. *So…*" Jake paused. "You want to help me out?"

"What?"

"Maybe you could check with the Foggy Bottom folks and see what Mitchell has on file with them?"

"That would be highly unusual."

"But you'll do it, right?"

Maddie sighed.

"And, wait…" Jake grabbed his notepad. He flipped through the pages. "Yeah. Check out a Monique Del La Croix, too."

"Who's that?"

"We're not really sure, but she showed up at Mitchell's apartment after he turned up dead."

"Yeah. Okay."

"So, do you think we'll get some *Federale* visitors soon?"

"I wouldn't be surprised."

"Great."

"Don't make this splash back on me," Maddie said.

"You know I won't."

"Yeah. I do."

~~~

Locomotive 3382

The Wabtec ET62AL locomotive was the lead engine pulling a westbound CSX intermodal train through East Cleveland at three o'clock in the morning.

After a long 14L whistle call, the engineer sat back in his chair once he cleared the road crossing. Ahead in the train headlight, a figure suddenly appeared in the middle of the tracks walking towards the locomotive.

The engineer sat up and pulled the whistle, reaching for the brake handles, even though he knew it was hopeless to stop the 150-car freight train to avoid the collision.

The screech of steel skidding on steel filled the cabin.

The engineer watched, waiting for the figure to leap from the tracks.

"Get out of the way—*get out of the way!*" he yelled over the roar of the twelve-cylinder diesel engine.

The man disappeared in front of the train.

The engineer felt nothing from the impact sitting in his chair.

A half-mile later the freight train finally came to a stop.

The engineer buried his head in his hands.

~~~

"I don't appreciate this. Not at all," said Puff. He stood his lean body up straight between the tracks with his hands on his hips and a plastic bag in his right hand. "Not one bit. Calling me out in the middle of the night like this."

"Top of the morning to you, too," Jake said as he and Kim stepped up beside the parked locomotive. "Sorry to disturb your beauty sleep."

"Idiots."

"Hey, Jake. How are you doing?" Puff's partner, Bob, asked. "This case yours?"

"So it seems."

Bob adjusted his glasses and pulled his stomach in a bit as he looked Kim up one side and down the other. "And you must be Jake's new partner, right?"

"This is Bob," Jake said. "And that's Puff over there. From the Mechanical shop."

"Nice to meet you. I'm Kim." She shook Bob's hand. When she finally pulled it away, she rubbed her fingers together, trying to work the grease out.

"Yeah, it's a bit messy around here," Bob said. "Hydraulic oil."

"Right."

"Anyways, he took a header on the front end of the engine here, Jake," Bob said. "Kind of a mess."

"There ain't nothing but a big old bag of spare parts strewn out all over this damn place." Puff squinted at Jake. "I'm tired of scraping up Dermaloy skin parts off the snout of this beast."

"Serial numbers?" Jake asked.

"We found his head," Bob said.

Puff held up a plastic bag with the robot's skull inside.

Kim stared at Puff and the head.

"It was smashed into the front rail," Bob said. "We should be able to get an A-VIN off of it from inside."

"Good. Let me know." Jake walked back toward the cruiser.

Kim stared at the robotic mess slathered on the front of the locomotive.

Jake stopped and looked back. "You coming?"

"Yeah…yeah," she said, slowly turning away.

"Nice to meet you, Kim," Bob said. "Make sure you stop down and see us sometime. Okay?"

Kim skipped awkwardly down the railway bed to catch up with Jake. She waved back over her shoulder.

"Are you going to help me here or not?" Puff asked.

"She's nice. I like her," Bob said.

"Idiots," Puff growled.

~~~

The Canvas

EC and Wally struck out with the first two names on the list of clients from Fat Tony's office. The bungalow in the Brooklyn neighborhood had been bought three years before, but the wife didn't know where the old owner had moved. The second address was an empty lot off West 44th Street.

They cut up to Detroit Avenue and drove to Battery Park along the lake.

"What do you think? Third time's a charm?" Wally asked.

"We'll see."

"Mr. Optimism."

They pulled into the complex of townhouses facing the lake and drove down to unit 18C.

"You know, why don't you stand back over there," Wally said.

"Why's that?"

"Because you look too much like a cop. Let me give it a try. What's this guy's name?"

"Robert Bennington. He goes by Robby." EC looked at the stylish townhouse. "Hmmm…no visible means of support."

"Okay. Give me a go." Wally held his hand out to keep EC back. He went up and pounded on the door. "Yo! Robbie. Come on, man, it's me, Wally."

Wally looked back and winked at his partner.

EC rolled his eyes.

There was some shuffling behind the door. "Who?"

"Yeah. Wally. Come on, open up." Wally pressed his face close to the peephole and smiled. "Let's get some lunch or something."

"Wally? You know—" The deadbolt unlatched. The door opened. "I don't know any…"

"Yeah, you do," Wally said, holding up his badge. "Wally, from downtown."

"*Officer…*" Robbie was skinny and almost six feet tall, maybe five-foot, eleven inches. He leaned against the inside door jamb, dressed in Levi's and an A-frame T-shirt. His shoulder-length hair was pulled back in a ponytail.

"Hey, nice place." Wally looked around him into the apartment. "You here alone?"

Robbie pulled at his goatee and eyeballed EC leaning against the front quarter panel of their Crown Vic. "What's it to you?"

"*Fat Tony.*"

Robbie stood up straight and stared back.

Wally stepped right up next to the doorstep. He whispered, "Yeah, your name came up in an investigation."

"That got taken care of, you hear me? Mr. Eliot made it all go away."

"Relax, man. Take it easy. Unless, of course, you had something to do with four dead bodies."

"What are you talking about?"

"Or we could take this conversation downtown…*you know?*" Wally smiled.

A woman stepped out of the apartment next door. She stopped to look at Robbie, then EC, then Wally.

Wally spread his sports jacket back with his hands to reveal the badge on his belt. "Morning, ma'am."

Robbie sneered. "Good morning, Mrs. Polanski."

"More trouble, Mr. Bennington? Again?"

"Trouble?" Wally looked at Mrs. Polanski, then back at Robbie.

"You guys, come in—just for a minute." Robbie turned and walked back into his apartment. "I got nothing to hide."

Wally shrugged at EC and followed him in.

"Mrs. Polanski." EC stepped up on the porch and followed Wally inside.

Robbie led them back to the kitchen area and stepped behind the counter. "So, how can I help you, *officers?*"

"This is a nice place," Wally said. "You rent or own?"

"It's all mine."

Wally looked out the back window at Edgewater Park and the lake. "Two bedrooms up?"

Robbie nodded.

"Middle of the morning and you're still hanging around. What kind of job do you have?"

"I work…at night."

"Yeah. Right." Wally looked at EC and shrugged.

"So, what did Mr. Eliot tell you?"

"There was no case file on you," EC said. "Why is that?"

"I don't know. He made it go away. That's what I paid him for. And it was a lot. But that's all I know."

"And what was *that* all about?"

"She said she was eighteen—she was in a bar, for crying out loud. Don't you guys check that stuff out?"

"Not my circus. Not my monkey," Wally said.

"So, what happened?" EC asked.

"Her dad was some corporate CEO muckety-muck, you know? And he wanted my head on a platter, but Mr. Eliot got involved and I guess he worked it all out somehow and the guy ended up dropping the charges."

"Because…" Wally said, "you're such an upstanding citizen right?"

"Something like that."

"And why did Fat Tony take your case?" EC asked.

"I got friends, you know? I know them. And they know him. That's all."

"Yeah, yeah, I get it."

"Where were you last Friday?" EC asked.

"Why?"

"That's when Fat Tony was killed," Wally said.

"Killed?"

"And you were…"

"Down in the Flats. With the guys, at Hoopples. But, Fat Tony's dead?"

"As a doornail," Wally said. "How late?"

"Til two. Then we played some poker. At a place in Ohio City. I got home at six—six-thirty." Robbie shook his head. "Man, there are going to be some people upset about this."

"Why's that?" EC asked.

"You know who he is, right? Who he works for, right?"

"The same guys as you, huh," EC said.

"So, if he's dead, then he didn't give me up, right?"
Wally shrugged.

"You got his files?"

"We need names. Of the guys at the club." Wally slid his notepad and a pen over to Robbie. "Write them down."

"Yeah. Sure." Robbie scribbled.

"You know a Mitchell Scofield?" Wally asked.

"No. Who's he?"
Wally sighed.
"You know anyone who wanted Fat Tony dead?" EC asked.
"No, man. He was protected. You know what I mean?"
"Well, not protected enough," Wally said.

~~~

Woody

Jake and Kim walked into the morgue.

Woody was hunched over Fat Tony's body behind a face shield, carving a Y into his torso. He stopped, closed his eyes, and breathed in deeply. "Kim…right?"

Jake shook his head and touched his nose. "He's got a Super Sniffer."

"And, of course, you, Jake. The aftershave with a ship on the bottle." Woody stood up. "So, good to see you again, Kim. You guys are just in time."

Jake slid on a pair of safety glasses. He pointed out a plastic bin on the wall with glasses for Kim, then went over next to the autopsy table. "So, how much?"

"Three ninety-two. And who is the big winner?"

"Wally had four-twelve. EC was at three-fifty."

"What about you?" Woody asked Kim.

"She didn't play." Jake shook his head. "I had three eighty-five."

"Seven, huh? Did you ever work the midway? Pick a prize—any prize," Woody said, waving at the wall of drawers holding refrigerated bodies.

"I'll take door number three, Monte," Jake said.

"Well, I could let you have what's behind that door right now." Woody pointed at the drawer labeled with a three. "Or

I'll offer you one hundred dollars or, maybe, the chance to win a new car."

"I'll take the hundred dollars," Jake said.

"Yeah…right." Woody looked at Kim. "He's just got no sense of adventure."

"I know. What a drag for me," Kim said. "Jesus, look at all those fat rolls."

Woody patted Fat Tony's blubber, then lifted his face mask and winked at Kim. He turned to Jake. "I like her. A lot."

"I'll alert the media," Jake said. "So, what do we have going on here with Fat Tony?"

"Just as I suspected: strangulation." Woody lowered his face shield and pulled open a flap over Fat Tony's larynx. "Crushed hyoid bone. Only one set of prints on his neck—fingers here on the left side and a thumbprint over on the right. That was one strong dude…"

"Or a synthoid," Jake said.

"Yeah, that's what I'm thinking," Woody said. "It's like the others—Burr, Whistler…and Scofield, too."

"The robot on the train tracks?" Kim asked.

Jake nodded. "Yeah. Probably."

"I heard about that. Did you guys get a hand? I can compare it to the prints," Woody said.

"Just the head. It kind of got splattered against a freight train engine."

"Eh, *que sera, sera.*" Woody shrugged. He peeled back the skin and muscles off Fat Tony's abdomen. He picked up a rib spreader. "You might want to stand back a bit."

"Wait a minute. What's that?" Jake pointed at a tattoo on the outside of Fat Tony's right bicep.

Motherless Children

"Besides the barcode, it's the only other mark on his body. I got a picture of it."

Jake leaned in close and looked. The tattoo was a pale blue spiraling triangle framed by another triangle. "Did you look this up?"

"I've been a little busy." Woody waved the rib spreader in his hands. "A coroner's work is never done."

"What is it?" Kim asked.

"We're going to need to take a much closer look at Mr. Eliot." Jake took his phone out and snapped a picture of the tattoo on Mr. Eliot's arm. He showed it to Kim. "You recognize this?"

Kim shook her head.

"He seems to have a preference for young boys," Jake searched on his iPhone. He held up an image from an FBI file.

"Let me see that," Woody said. "Ugh! What a worm."

"Anything on Burr, Whistler, or Scofield?" Jake asked.

"Whistler was all tattooed up, but I don't recall anything like that. You'd have to check the autopsy photos," Woody said. "Burr was clean. Figures, he was an accountant. Scofield had a small Yin-Yang symbol on his back. That's it."

"So, Fat Tony was expunging sex offenders?" Kim asked.

"Maybe. But that doesn't explain Scofield. He's clean," Jake said.

"So far," Kim said.

"Anyway, this conversation has been enlightening," Woody raised the rib spreader. "But the work is really piling up around here."

"You want to watch the rest of this?" Jake asked.

"I think I'm good," Kim said.

"Woody, you've been a gracious host," Jake said. "But we're

heading back to the Alley. Send over your report when it's done."

"Come back anytime—especially you, Kim."

~~~

Follow the Money

"You got a minute?" Q asked Jake as he waited outside the doorway into Exit Alley.

"What's up?"

Q looked at Kim. "It's kind of a personal thing."

Jake shrugged.

"You boys knock yourselves out." She went in.

"What?"

Q walked up the alley. "Found it."

"The four hundred and fifty million?"

"In a Cayman Islands account."

"So…good. Right?"

"Maybe. Maybe not." Q stopped in the shadows between the buildings. He lowered his voice. "Remember, we thought it was the Baron who did it, right? Well, it's been moving around since he took the big dive off the Main Avenue Bridge."

"Moving?"

"He's dead, right? You're sure?"

"Yeah. They fished him out of the lake." Jake stepped up close to Q. "Then, who is doing this?"

"Well, that's kind of the beauty of bitcoins. All anonymous. And the Caymans are like Switzerland. Numbered accounts and such. Nobody knows—not even the banks."

"But you know, right?"

Q shook his head.

"What do you mean moving?"

"It's complicated. But the four hundred and fifty million got broken up and moved around to different crypto exchanges, then reassembled in the island account. So I started pinging away at the hash codes, right? Then…"

"Then, what?"

"Money started moving out. Not much, really. I think maybe forty or fifty thousand dollars' worth, so far."

"Who?"

"Yeah…*who?*"

"Where's it going?" Jake asked.

"Another good question."

"But you're looking into it, right?"

Q nodded.

Jake glanced up the alley at the District House, then back towards the entrance to Exit Alley. "What about the barcodes?"

Q shrugged. "Nothing in any of the usual databases so far."

"You milking us on this?"

"No. I can multitask, you know."

Jake pulled his iPhone out of his pocket. He showed the tattoo from Fat Tony to Q. "You know what that is?"

"Is that…"

"You've seen it before, right?"

"Yeah. Kind of a stranger-danger thing at the skateboard parks when I was young. You know? Is that what this case is all about?"

"I don't know." Jake shook his head. "I don't know."

Q stuffed his hands in his pockets and kicked at rocks on the ground.

"There's a guy, named Anthony Eliot. He's a lawyer—or was. Look into him, okay?"

"What am I looking for?"

"This." Jake held up his phone.

Q nodded.

"And see if you can find out where that fifty-thousand dollars went to. Okay?"

"Sure."

"Thanks." Jake nodded and started walking towards the House.

"Where are you going?"

"I got to talk to Sands about this."

"He won't like it."

"None of us do."

*****~~~*****

Cutty's

Jake waited in his booth at the back of Cutty's Deli. He decided his conversation with Lt. Sands would be best held outside of the House.

"What are you up to, Jake?" Cutty came up to the table and asked, sipping scotch out of his CPD coffee mug. "Sitting here all alone and all."

"Eh…waiting for Sands."

Cutty took another sip. He scanned the tables in the deli, then sat down across from Jake. He leaned in. "How's your *new* partner working out? Huh?"

Jake shrugged.

"Six guys went down in Narcotics. And she skated."

"Yup. Skated into a cushy, dead-end job in the Geek Squad…just like me."

Cutty sat back. "She didn't throw in with Internal Affairs?"

"Seems not."

"So she says. Or is she after you now?"

"I'm clean…*mostly.*"

Cutty squinted at Jake over another sip of scotch. *"Mostly* don't cut it with IA."

Lt. Sands walked up and stood behind Cutty.

Cutty stared at Jake. He nodded slowly, then curled his lip. "Think about it."

Lt. Sands looked at Jake and frowned.

Cutty slid out of the booth and stood up. He took a sip of scotch. "Lt. Sands. It's been a little while."

"Well, you know…the job and all."

"Have a seat."

"I'm not interrupting anything, am I?"

"Nah. Me and Jake—just going over old times. You know?"

"Yeah. Sure." Lt. Sands sat down.

"What'll you have?" Cutty asked.

"Just some coffee. Thanks."

Cutty put his hand on Lt. Sands' shoulder. "Look after this one, okay? He's *mostly* a good guy. You know?"

"Ah…sure."

Cutty headed back to the counter and told Emma to get Lt. Sands a cup of coffee.

She came over, set it down, and sneered at Jake.

He shook her off.

"So…what was that all about?" Lt. Sands asked after Emma left.

"He doesn't like Kim."

Lt. Sands took a sip of coffee. "And you?"

"She's a pain in the ass. Made me pay for my cannoli."

"What a crime. And that's why you asked me down here?"

Jake shook his head. He looked around the deli, then back at Lt. Sands. "What do you want me to do with this case?"

"Well, you should probably try to solve it, I guess. That'd generally be a good thing."

Jake nodded. "And if it leads down some dark paths?"

"Dark? How dark?"

Jake held up his phone with the picture of Fat Tony's tattoo. Lt. Sands winced.

"Yeah. Little boys, I guess."

"And what does this have to do with the Senator's son?"

"I don't know. Eliot was a lawyer and he's connected to the first two vics. They were his clients. Sex crimes."

Lt. Sands looked away from the photo, down into his coffee.

"You really want me to solve this one?"

"Who else knows about this?"

"Kim and Woody." Jake paused. "And Q."

"Q?"

"He'll figure it out. All of it. If that's where you want to go."

Lt. Sands let out a big sigh. He looked at Jake. "You keep this under wraps, okay? Nobody else needs to know."

"I've got to tell EC and Wally."

"Yeah. Yeah. Of course." Lt. Sands pushed his coffee mug into the middle of the table. "You hold back your DD-5s on this—better yet, it'd be best if nothing finds its way into the system. Keep it in your notepads. If you know what I mean."

Jake nodded.

"Keep me in the loop—all the way." Lt Sands stood up. "And nothing goes to Public Square. Got it? Send everything my way."

"You bet, boss."

"Anything else I need to know about?"

Jake thought for a moment but shook his head.

"You're paying for this, right?"

Jake looked up and gave him a big grin.

"Yeah, I don't want to know," Lt. Sands said as he turned and left.

Jake called EC and told him about Fat Tony's tattoo and to get a search warrant for his apartment.

~~~

Detecting

Q stood outside the doorway to the conference room in Exit Alley and watched Detective Kim's back through the window beside the door as she poured through stacks of papers. His laptops sat across the table, searching. He wasn't worried: the screens were locked.

He sighed. Finally, he went in. "Oh…hey."

Kim looked up. "Where's Jake?"

"He, ah, went to talk to Lt. Sands for a minute." Q went around the table and sat down across from Kim. He watched her flip through the pages. "What are you working on?"

"I'm going through the phone LUDs, trying to find a connection between Eliot and Mitchell Scofield."

"Any luck?"

Kim shook her head. "There has got to be something. Somewhere."

"Yeah…somewhere." Q unlocked the screen of the police department laptop. "The guy's a creep, huh."

Kim looked up from the papers she was holding. "What?"

"Eliot. And little boys…you know, his pedo tattoo."

"Jake told you?"

"Yeah. He showed me outside. These guys are always all kinds of dirty on the Internet. So, I guess he wants me to see if I can track something on him that way."

"Oh…"

"As long as I don't have to get my hands dirty, I'm okay with that."

Kim put the papers down. "So, what was your crime?"

"Crime?"

"You used to work here, right? But not anymore."

Q rubbed his right eye. "Yeah, well, I guess I didn't exactly follow *protocol.*"

"What does that mean?"

"On our last big case—the one with that Baron guy—we found his server farm in the Flats he used to reprogram the synthoids. It was supposed to be taken off the grid, but, I, ah, put it back online."

"But you found him, right?"

"Well, actually, he found me. Working there."

"Oh…"

"Then he bleached it all." Q stared off into the space over Kim's head. "Everything that was on the servers…It was really kind of elegant if you ask me. He had created a digital copy of the mind in all those silicon chips—right brain, left brain, thinking, dreaming, feelings—everything. And I was just getting to the bottom of things."

"But he found out about you and erased it."

"Yeah. Yeah, he did. So, I guess it was a good thing that Maddie just put him down."

"Maddie?"

"Ten shots to the chest."

"Ouch."

"He tumbled off the Main Avenue Bridge into the river. And that was that."

"And you got booted from the department."

Q nodded.

"But now you're back."

"Yeah, it's what I do now…I consult—mostly as a white hat—hacking for corporations to find their vulnerabilities so they can lace them up."

"Mostly?"

"I don't work for you guys anymore. You know?"

"What does that mean?"

Q smiled.

Kim smiled back. "And why do you have two laptops?"

"This one is mine," Q said.

"Yeah, why?"

"Why what?"

"You are working on the case, right? And you've got the laptop that EC got you. Why do you need your laptop here, too?"

"I, ah…"

"What's on there?"

"It's personal."

"Show me."

"Yeah, I don't think so." Q pulled the screen down on his laptop, putting it into sleep mode.

Jake came into the conference room. He looked at the staredown between Kim and Q. "So…what am I missing here?"

"Oh, nothing," Kim and Q said together—not so innocently.

Kim smiled at Q.

He returned half a grin.

Kim picked up her papers again, glaring at Q.

Q opened the police department laptop screen, staring back.

"Yeah, okay, whatever—now about the case…" Jake said.

He went over to the murder board and stared at the pictures. "Q…the barcodes…what have you got?"

"Still searching, man."

Jake turned around and looked at Q.

"They don't fit any of the obvious choices—products, ISBNs, bank accounts, arrest records or court dockets or anything. I know there's something there, but…"

Jake shook his head. He looked at Kim. "Come on, let's get out of here."

"Where?"

"The other two crime scenes. Have you been to them?"

Kim shook her head.

"Then, let's go take a look, okay?"

"In your car?"

"Come on, you'll get used to it. And grab your iSlate." Jake stopped at the door and turned back to Q. "What if they don't relate to a thing?"

"Yeah, okay, but what?"

Jake shrugged his shoulders. "That's what you're getting paid for."

"Gee, thanks. But that doesn't really help."

Jake headed out the door.

Kim got up and chased after him. When she caught up with Jake on the way to the parking lot, she asked, "So, what is it about this stupid car?"

"You need to relax a bit, you know? Enjoy life a little. Let the wind blow back your hair."

"That's so *old school.*" She walked around to the other side of Jake's Mustang. "We're not teenagers, you know."

"It'd be nice, though. Wouldn't it? Not a care in the world.

Soak it in, Kim. Soak it in for just a minute or two."

Jake got in and fired up the engine. He rev'd it up a couple of times.

Kim shook her head and got in. "You're like a child sometimes."

"Yeah. Sometimes." Jake pulled out and found his way to Lake Avenue, then onto the Shoreway, heading for Edgewater Park.

On the Main Avenue Bridge, Kim asked, "Is that where you got him? The Baron?"

Jake nodded, staring straight ahead.

"Or should I say, Maddie got him."

Jake looked over at Kim. "She's a hell of a shot."

Kim smiled and gazed out over the lake.

Jake grabbed his phone and hit play, sending Bruce Springsteen's "Thunder Road" through the car stereo.

Kim closed her eyes and shook her head. She smiled just a little bit.

Jake turned the music up.

They came down the hill past the beach on the right.

"So, why does Q have two laptops?" Kim raised her voice and asked.

"I guess one is his."

"Yeah...*why?*"

Jake eyeballed Kim out of the side of his eye.

"He's got the police laptop from EC, right? What's he doing with the MacBook? What does he need that for?"

"I don't know. What do you think?"

"He's looking for something else."

"Oh, yeah? What's that?"

"I don't know. I don't know." Kim turned and looked at Jake. "What do you think?"

Jake accelerated up the hill and veered off on the Lake Road exit. He turned right into the Metropark and rolled to a stop, sideways across the empty parking lot lines.

"What's he looking for?" Kim asked as Jake shut down the car.

"I don't know," Jake said. "Did you ask him?"

"I did."

"And what did he say?"

"He didn't."

"So, you're being kind of nosy, then." Jake got out of the car. He turned back to Kim. *"Gladys…"*

"I'm *detecting*, damn it." Kim got out and came around next to Jake. "You know. Don't you."

Jake looked at Kim, trying to decide whether Cutty was right or not—whether she was working with Internal Affairs.

Kim cocked her head to look into Jake's eyes. "You *do* know…"

"Yeah. I do." Jake smiled. "And it's none of our business."

"But you don't care—"

"Nope." Jake turned and headed over towards the statue of Richard Wagner.

Kim watched Jake walk around behind the statue. She slowly came over. When she started to speak, Jake held up his hand to quiet her.

"This is where Whistler, the chef, was found. Leaning against the back of the statue."

"So, was he killed here or just dumped here?" Kim asked.

Jake looked around. "I think he was killed here. In the park."

"What was he doing in the park?"

"Good question."

"I'd guess he was meeting someone."

Jake nodded. "After the restaurant closed."

"Yeah, that's not suspicious."

"For what? Drugs? Sex?"

Kim looked up at the top of the statue. "Three in the morning? My guess would be sex."

"What did they ping him on?"

Kim checked her iSlate. "Got caught with an underaged girl."

"Hmmm…at three in the morning? In the park?" Jake shook his head. "That's not stacking up."

"Well, maybe he loves opera." Kim motioned towards the Richard Wagner statue.

"Yeah, I think I'd kill myself."

"Me, too."

Jake smiled. "So we have something in common."

"I'm feeling the love."

"Pull up the crime scene photos." Jake walked over next to Kim and watched over her shoulder.

She slid slowly through the photos.

"Hey, stop. Go back."

She slid back a picture.

"What's that?" Jake pointed at a step van parked in the background.

She zoomed in. The truck was painted orange with paisley patterns wrapped around the front end and trailing along the sides like colorful flames. It said "Iris & Dolly's Bistro" on the side.

"That's his food truck right?" Jake asked.

"Yeah. So?"

"He drives a Corvette, though, right?"

"Yeah…*another one*—like you and your Mustang, huh?" Kim rolled her eyes. "But, yeah…in the middle of the night?

In the park? For sex? He brings his food truck?"

"Iris…Iris and Dolly…*Iris—yeah, that's it.*"

"What?"

"God, why didn't I think of it? Iris—*from the movies.*"

"Who is Iris?"

"Yeah, yeah, yeah—*Taxi Driver*—Jody Foster. But who is Dolly?"

"What movie?" Kim asked. "You've got to help me out here."

"Come on. Martin Scorsese's classic. She was the underaged prostitute that Travis Bickel was obsessed with." Jake wandered off a bit. He thought for a minute. "Just for drill, look up Lolita on your iSlate."

Kim tapped. "What? The book?"

Jake walked over. He clicked on the link for Nabokov's novel in Wikipedia, scrolled down, and read. "There, Delores Haze, also variably known as Dolly, Lo, Lola…*Lolita.*"

"Oh, so she lied on her job application. *Right.*" Kim said. "Maybe Whistler wasn't so innocent after all."

"And the food truck…"

"He was here to pick something up. What?"

"Motherless children…"

~~~

The Flatiron Building

Fat Tony's apartment was on the top floor of the downtown Flatiron Building, facing out over the Theater District. Jake stood at the window, looking down on the huge outdoor chandelier hanging over the intersection of Euclid Avenue and East 14th Street. It was beginning to glow in the dusk. The marquis for the Ohio and State theaters came on.

"So, what are we looking for?" Wally asked as he stepped up next to Jake, pulling on a set of latex gloves. He looked back around at the living room.

"You know…"

"Ugh."

"Yeah."

"Man, this place is just a…"

"A mess," Jake said.

"He kind of gives hoarders a bad name, you know? My sister is one and even she would be appalled."

Jake was standing in the only clear area in the room, next to a huge, overstuffed leather chair, an ottoman, and a large end table in front of the sharp-cornered windows facing east. The rest of the living room was filled with haphazardly stacked moving boxes, banker's boxes, stacks of papers, piles of stuffed manila folders, and magazines. An odd assortment of trinkets, pictures, cheap souvenirs, and more expensive *objects de art,* were scattered around on the tables and box lids. Nothing was hanging on the walls. There did not seem to be any apparent pattern in style, theme, or cost of the items.

Wally scratched the side of his head. "We're going to be here all night, you know."

"Yup."

"What do you think he pays in rent for this place?"

"Nothing a cop could afford." Jake turned around.

"You gotta ask, you know? And I get curious."

Jake looked over at Kim, who searched the kitchen cabinets. "Well, it should be available soon."

"You are hilarious."

"Yeah. I know." Jake grinned at Wally.

They got to work, opening banker's boxes and digging through the contents. While the room was a haphazard mess, the boxes were filled with the minutia of Fat Tony's life, organized in manila file folders. One box held detailed records of the maintenance and gas mileage of every car he had owned since he was sixteen, in chronological order. Several more boxes contained all of his receipts, divided up into in-store, online, and Amazon purchases. Another few boxes held a myriad of physician discharge papers, lab results, billing records, and insurance payouts, for his regular visits to the Cleveland Clinic for a long series of ineffectual efforts to find some medical malady afflicting Fat Tony—besides his obvious obesity.

Jake went through box after box of books organized by categories: biographies, self-help, and, oddly, the history of armed conflict separated into eras starting with the Civil War, World War I, World War II, Vietnam, and the more recent modern Middle East Crusades. He flipped through the pages, though few of the book jackets showed any sign of having been cracked from reading.

They moved steadily through the boxes, stacking them in the space by the overstuffed chair when done.

Kim searched the one uncluttered room: the kitchen. The counters were cleared and the sink and dishwasher were empty. All the dishes, pans, and flatware were neatly stacked in the cabinets and drawers. There were no cans or boxes of food in the pantry. Kim worked her way finally to the refrigerator and stared at the door.

"It's not going to search itself," Wally called out to Kim, looking at her from the living room.

"Come on. Don't be a wuss," Jake said. "I'm sure it's okay."

Kim gave them a scorning look.

Jake and Wally stood watching.

Kim took a deep breath and opened the refrigerator door. She looked inside and saw dozens and dozens of plastic, paper, and styrofoam to-go boxes stacked up from the bottom to the top. She drew a quick breath, scowled, then slammed the door shut.

"I think I'll go help EC search the bedroom." Kim headed quickly to the front of the apartment, shaking her head and breathing through her mouth.

Jake and Wally laughed.

In the bedroom, EC neatly lay out photographs on the bedsheets.

"What's going on in here?" Kim asked.

"These were in shoeboxes under the bed," EC said softly.

Kim stepped over to look and groaned. "And I thought the refrigerator was creepy."

EC kept laying down photos of young boys, aged eight to, maybe, fourteen in neat rows. He carefully matched the photo sizes—wallet-sized, four-by-six, five-by-sevens, and odd-sized squares in carefully arranged stacks. Some looked like family photos. Some were school pictures and some were magazine and catalog cutouts. "You know what's weird?"

"Hey, Jake. Hey, Wally," Kim called out. "You might want to see this."

"They're all…ah, fully clothed." EC looked over at Kim with a curious look on his face.

Jake and Wally came in and walked over to the bed.

"Jesus." Wally shook his head.

"Yeah, there's boxes and boxes of them," said EC, pointing at the shoe boxes stacked on the bed.

"No electronics? Anywhere in the apartment?" Jake asked.

"No. Nothing," Kim said.

"No phone?"

"Not here. We got one at the crime scene, but there were no pictures, or texts, or even any email links. Nothing," said Wally.

EC went back to sorting out pictures.

"Did the tech guys come back with any Internet browsing history?" Jake asked.

"Nothing for Fat Tony." Wally shook his head.

"What about Scofield?"

"We're still waiting for it," EC said.

"Waiting for it?" asked Kim. "Why's that?"

"Well, when your father is a U.S. Senator…"

"What does that have to do with anything?"

Jake just gestured towards EC's neat stacks of photos. "Maybe…"

~~~

The Butcher Shop

A rusted I-beam girder hung high across the top of the small room in the back of an abandoned butcher shop on Lorain Boulevard near West 41st Street. Crudely, a pair of chains hung down shoulder-width apart with meat hooks on the end, holding up an inert synthoid beneath its shoulders. The front and back torso panels were removed exposing a rat's nest of wires and modules in the abdomen. The Lithium-Dioxide fuel cells were stacked neatly beneath the robot's dangling feet.

He worked slowly and methodically, undoing small Phillip's head screws. They clinked softly as he dropped them into a magnetic metal container on the workbench to his side. He carefully slid out an electronic module and let it dangle by the wires, then began again with the screwdriver.

He hummed a meandering melody—a scattershot collection of the bits and pieces of songs streamed on his phone, connected without meaning or merit. Just noise to fill the quiet of the slaughterhouse.

A different kind of murder board was laid out on the wall across from the workbench. A spiderweb of twine strings stretched from the happy, smiling photograph of a young teenage girl holding a field hockey stick and dressed in a dark blue uniform trimmed in sky blue out to mugshot of Robbie Bennington, then to an X-ed out photo of Fat Tony lying dead on the railroad tracks and, from him to Alan Burr, dead in an alley in the Warehouse District, and Paul Whistler leaning back lifeless against the statue of Richard Wagner in Edgewater Park. Alone and above the other photos, Mitchell Scofield's body, leaned against a dumpster in AsiaTown. All of the dead victims had photos of their barcodes taped beneath their headshots. Twine strings led out from Scofield's photo right into a semicircle of four empty squares—except for the one in the top. In it was a picture of Monique De La Croix.

His was an old-fashioned way of Munchausing, reprogramming, and replacing modules buried deep inside the chassis of older, less integrated synthoids. It gave him a kind of pleasure, working with his hands on actual hardware. Perhaps there was more risk, but, on the other hand, once done, his murderbots were completely untethered from himself and the Atlas grid, having been re-assembled out of a menagerie of parts like some kind of Frankensteins.

It was surprisingly easy to find the gray and black markets of parts for modifying the old robots. Lots of less profitable companies and underfunded government agencies—like his own Street Department—ran the old Gen 1 systems long past their expected expiration dates. None of the OEMs made replacement parts—they were pushing their new improved systems with enhanced features and more advanced technologies. So, scavengers found their way into the marketplace to keep the old originals running—some with authorized parts and some with more creative ways to get what was needed. And that was how he found Mitchell Scofield's consulting firm, A.V Meridian, on the peripheries of that world and how the Senator's face and barcode found their way onto his murder board.

Deep inside the thorax, he found the tiny black box of

firmware chipsets that formed the BCU—Behavioral Control Unit. It was easier that way in the manufacturing process in case the OEM intended the synthoid to be acquired by a military unit, where the limits on harm inflicted towards human beings were much less restricted.

He pulled the module out, disconnected its Molex connector, then replaced it with an equivalent unit—much more difficult to locate and acquire in the Darknet black markets, smuggled into the United States from a Russian infantry robot—one originally programmed to ignore the First Law.

He meticulously reassembled the internals of the synthoid, carefully rerouting the wires back around the modules as he went. The Lithium-Diode fuel cells were replaced and reattached. The abdominal cover panel locked in place with a battery-driven screwdriver.

He smiled, pleased with his work.

The city street sweeper stepped to the workbench and picked up several stacks of cellophaned hundred dollar bills he found slipped through the mail slot in the front door of the meat market. It appeared to be at least fifty thousand dollars.

He wondered who had put it there.

The Fourth Laws

Jake sat alone at his kitchen table drinking his morning coffee.

"So…that was fun. No?" Kristi from Five Alive News asked, as she strolled in tying her oriental bathrobe tight around her waist. She poured herself a cup of coffee and leaned against the kitchen counter.

He nodded. "Mmm. *Delightful.*"

"You bet your ass it was." She kicked the back of Jake's chair.

He turned and ran his eyes up and down over her curvaceous body, and back up again. Her hair was still wet from the shower. A rivulet of water dripped slowly from the ends down between her breasts. Jake thought she looked much better without the heavy hairspray and the carefully sculpted makeup put on for the cameras.

She let him look for a little while.

"You look nice that way," Jake said.

"What way is that?"

"Kind of…wholesome."

"Yeah, but wholesome doesn't really sell now, does it."

"Well, it works for me."

She ran her hand back slowly through her blonde hair. "So, now what?"

"What, what?"

"Sleeping with the enemy, right?"

Jake gave a crooked smile.

"You…are a bit *incorrigible.*"

"It comes with the territory."

Kristi hid her smile behind a sip of coffee.

"And think I pretty much got what I wanted." Jake winked at Kristi. "What is it that the enemy wants from me?"

"Well…"

"Okay. What?"

"Well, your case…have you heard from the FBI yet? I mean, he is a senator's son."

Jake shook his head. "No. Nothing."

"What's the old man up to, then? You'd think he'd be all over you about Mitchell's murder. What is he hiding?"

"Hiding?"

"He's a politician. They genetically can't keep their mouths shut about anything. Unless…"

Jake's phone rang. He looked at the screen. It was Maddie.

Kristi frowned. "Work?"

Jack sighed.

"Oh well, too bad—*oh, so sad.*" She stepped over and ran her hand across his cheek, then sauntered down the hall towards the bedroom. "We'll talk more later—maybe you should get that."

"Mmm…"

She stopped at the doorway and pouted his way. "All play and no work…"

Jake answered the phone. "Yeah?"

Silence on the other end.

Kristi blew him a kiss and went into the bedroom.

"Maddie?"

"I didn't get you up, did I?"

"What's going on?"

The line was quiet. "Where are you, working the case?"

"Some headway. There's definitely a sexual thing going on." Jake looked down the hallway towards his bedroom. "Not sure how it connects all the players yet—especially with Scofield. And, of course, the player to be named later. What did you find out about the Senator's boy?"

"His company, A.V. Meridian, is set up as a sub-chapter S corporation. Mitchell holds the majority of shares. Del la Croix owns a piece, as does his uncle."

"And the Senator?"

"Not listed. And they seem to be doing quite well for themselves. Nine figures worth on the income side of things. But they also seem to have quite a lot of expenses."

"And what are they doing to create that income?"

"Not exactly sure, but the income stream is decidedly from U.S.-based companies—or at least shell corporations. I haven't been able to find anything out at the State Department."

"And the expenses?"

"Not exactly sure, either. There seem to be a lot of trips to Hong Kong, Thailand, and mainland China, but I really need to get my hands on their books."

"And that's not going to happen, right?"

"Not with the seventh floor upstairs involved."

Jake nodded to himself. "Okay."

"But the sexual thing in your case. Does it, ah, have to do with…"

"Young boys and girls, it seems. The lawyer, Fat Tony, was tattooed up with it. I'll bet the mob didn't know about that."

"Maybe they're getting a little more…enlightened."

"And he helped the victim who was the chef beat the wrap on an underaged girl."

"You know…" Maddie cleared her throat. "There is an unwritten Fourth Law."

"What is it?"

"At least in this country. In other places—places where, say, there might be…restrictions on families."

"Like China?"

"Maybe. Anyway, the U.S. doesn't allow…young, underaged synthoids."

"Underaged?"

"It's definitely a no-no. Nothing under twenty-one."

"Oh…"

From down the hall, Kristi called out, "Are you *still* on the phone? It's my day off, you know."

Silence on the line.

"I better let you go." Maddie hung up.

~~~

Oxbow Bend

Q loped lazily around the oxbow bend in the Cuyahoga River downtown, taking the path of most resistance, vaulting retaining walls, climbing up and around and over iron bridge trestles, and jumping completely up and down over stairways, sometimes using center handrails with his feet in a perfectly timed stride to extend his leap. He was circling his quarry.

He slowed to a stop and stared across the way at the three-story warehouse building in The Flats once occupied by Whitechapel LLC. With the death of the Baron, it was abandoned now. He caught his breath, then walked slowly towards it. He dug in his pocket for the key he made at the time. Though he had not been back inside since the night the Baron was killed, he regularly traced his parkour course around the bend with it in view.

He went around to the front door. The police notices marking the building as a crime scene were long gone now. He tried the door. It was locked, but his key still worked. He climbed up the stairs to the second-floor server room. The racks were all empty and tangled with disconnected Cat5e cables, the servers and RAID drives seized and sitting in an evidence warehouse somewhere. It smelled musty, still with a hint of ozone in the air. A dim light fought its way into the room through windows frosted with dust. Chairs were scattered haphazardly around the conference tables and desks, littered with papers unrelated to the investigation. The police had taken the pictures of the victims taped to the wall into evidence, leaving ghostly white squares on the plaster.

He slowly walked up and down the aisles between the racks, recalling the hours he spent, night after night, with his laptop plugged into the Black Tier, trying to decode the programming of the Invisible Mind within it…before it was erased.

He still had the text saved on his phone from that night after the Baron wiped the data drives clean:

My Dear Companion — Thank you so much for keeping me company, but the time has come for me to be on my way. Attached is the encryption key to what you seek, but, alas, there is no longer much to find there. Not even breadcrumbs. Until we mee again, warmest regards, the Baron.

An error of hubris, keeping the server farm connected to the world, led to Q's firing from Exit Alley.

Although he was long dead, Q felt the bitcoin movements in the Cayman Island account were somehow linked back to the Baron's digital recreations of past serial killers with cyber hacked synthoids.

But who? he wondered.

Q recalled his testimony at the hacker trials from the DI-7 channel labeled JtR-Overlords—JtR for Jack the Ripper—who were caught at the warehouse on the night of the SWAT raid. They all went to jail, not that any of them had the wherewithal to steal the crypto keys for four-hundred fifty million dollars from a law firm's secured delivery synthoid.

What happened to Amy—the young Amy?

Jake's waitress girlfriend from the diner had been thrown off the Main Avenue Bridge that night by a synthoid and died hitting the river a hundred feet below. Maddie had placed the younger girl in a foster home in Westlake before she left for the FBI in Washington DC.

But she was too young, Q thought. *Or was she?*

Numerology

Wally sat waiting in a booth at the Golden Phoenix Chinese restaurant in Lakewood.

His notebook lay open on the table and he stared at the barcode numbers written down from the victims, trying to make sense of them. He wrote the number from Mitchell Scofield out on his paper napkin: 7 7928 73444 5.

He tapped it with his pen and shook his head.

"What's that?" Amanda asked stepping up behind him.

"Huh? Oh, just numbers."

"Important?"

"I don't know. Supposedly…but nobody knows what they mean."

"Hmm." She pushed Wally in towards the wall with her hips and sat down.

Wally sat himself up straight. "Kind of cozy, no?"

"You don't mind, do you, big guy?"

He smiled. "No. Make yourself at home."

"Yeah. I will. What are you going to do? Write me a ticket?"

Wally shook his head. "You know I could."

"Okay. So, what are these numbers? From a case?"

"I shouldn't talk about it—"

"About what?"

"It's a murder case."

"And you don't know what they mean?"

"Nope."

"Let me see."

"I really shouldn't…"

She gave him a stern scowl. *"Wally!"*

He pushed the napkin in front of Amanda. He propped his head on his hand and looked out the window.

"And so?"

"It was found tattooed with a barcode on a murder victim."

"Who?"

"Mitchell Scofield. Remember? The Senator's son?"

"Oh, yeah. So, what's his birthday?"

Wally checked his notebook. "August 14—"

"Oh, a Leo…" Amanda took Wally's pen and circled the last number: 5. "Okay. Here. Let me see, now."

"Huh?"

"What's his middle name?"

Wally checked his notebook again.

"Oh, give me that." Amanda slid it over in front of her.

"But it's a murder investigation. You shouldn't be seeing that."

"Hang on a second." Amanda read the notes. "Okay, Chase."

Amanda listed out the numbers: 4, 1, 4, 3, 5, 5, 3, and 3, then added them up to 28, then circled the fourth and fifth numbers. She listed and added 3, 5, 1, 3, and 5. She circled the 17.

"What are you doing?" Wally asked.

"Hush a minute, already."

Amanda listed 3, 3, 7, 8, 1, 5, 3, and 4 to 34. She circled the next two numbers. She added 28, 17, and 34 to 79. She added 7 and 9 to 16. Then she wrote seven beneath them. She circled the first number: 7. "Easy-peasy. It's Chaldean Numerology."

"What?"

"Oh, you…it's a witches thing, you know?"

"What's that mean?"

"I'm hungry—you're buying right?"

Wally looked at Amanda and held his hands up.

She smiled.

"Yes. Of course. It's my treat."

"Good."

Wally waved the waitress over. "Szechuan Chicken. Extra spicy. With fried rice and an egg roll."

"Always the same thing, huh."

"I know what I like. And you?"

"Let me see…let me see." Amanda traced her finger through the menu.

"You eat here all the time."

"Okay. Okay. General Tso's Chicken, please. And Crab Rangoon—you'll have some of that, right?"

Wally nodded.

"Thank you," Amanda said to the waitress. Amanda poured herself green tea.

"So, what is this Chaldean Numerology?"

"It's ancient Babylonian from over five thousand years ago."

"And how do you know that's what this is?"

"Well, first of all, Chaldean uses the person's birthdate—here, five. Remember he was born on August 14." She pointed at the last number at the end of the barcode. "You add the one and the four together to get five. The Kabbalah system only uses the person's name. It's Hebrew. The Pythagorean system lists their numbers sequentially and uses the number nine. A-B-C-D-E-F-

G-H-I—Nine, right? Here in Mitchell's first name, it's a one, here. Chaldeans believe the number nine is sacred. And when you add it all up, you get twenty-eight. Here." She pointed to the circle around the fourth and fifth numbers in the barcode.

"Okay…"

"So whoever did this is using compound numbers. The Pythagorean System boils everything down to single digits. Simple. Right?"

Wally turned and leaned back against the wall. He frowned and looked at Amanda. "Really? Numerology?"

"I'm sure of it. Where's our food. I'm hungry."

"What does this all mean?"

"Oh, it's complicated. The Chaldeans believe the universe is built by vibrations and all those vibrations also have different frequencies, which is what the different numbers are all about. So, you have to sit down and figure out what everything means."

"How?"

"You interpret the numbers and maybe use Tarot Cards and astrology and dreams to sort things out for sure."

"So this guy is a witch?"

"Probably not, but he's definitely into numerology. That's for sure. And I'll tell you what. The forty-four in the number there—that's a karmic number. It's the number that holds the most power to shift your destiny down the light path or the dark path."

"The dark path…"

"Well, he's dead, isn't he?"

"Yes. Yes, he is."

"Can you do these other barcodes?"

"Give me the information and I'll do them at the store later. Let's not talk shop anymore, okay?"

"Yeah. Yeah, okay."

~~~

Internal Affairs

The clicks of Kim's high heels on the asphalt slowed as she approached her car in the police department parking lot. The frame of her red Kia Soul was only dimly lit in the night, as the street lamps in the corner where she parked were out. She looked up at them, then noticed a man leaning back against the tailgate. His features were hidden in the darkness.

Kim's hand slowly moved to the Glock 17 at her side.

"Hey now, Kim. There's no need for that."

Kim stopped thirty feet away. Her right hand gripped her pistol.

The man held his empty hands out to the side. "This is a bit far away to have a friendly conversation."

"Friendly?"

"Come on. We're on the same side, you know."

"And what side is that?" Kim asked.

"Truth…Justice…and…" The man stood up straight and gazed up at the darkened street lamps. He stepped forward and looked at Kim. "…the American Way."

Kim stared at the man's smiling Chinese face. *"American?"*

He shrugged and smiled.

"How many times have I told you? *No.* "

"Oh, let's just forget about all that—"

"All *that?*" Kim couldn't resist taking a few steps forward.

She pointed her finger at him. "That's why I'm here in Exit Alley, *dammit.*"

"In the midst of chaos, there is also opportunity." He moved close to her. He stood at attention and lowered his voice. "Did you really think you could ever become Chief of Police? Or even a District Commander?"

Kim stared back into his eyes. "I could have…*once.*"

"Yes. Once."

She pushed him aside with her shoulder, stepping towards the driver's door.

He turned to look at her. "The case—*your case*…the Senator's son…"

Kim stopped.

He relaxed his back. He smiled. "People are interested."

She turned to face him. "Who?"

"People. Important ones. People who can make things happen."

"Like what?"

"Your partner, Jake. You know he shot a councilman's son."

"He was cleared on that shoot. *Your people* did that a long time ago."

"Well…" He rubbed his chin with the back of his fingers. He closed his eyes. "And where is he now?"

Kim took a deep breath. "Better a diamond with a flaw than a pebble without."

He looked at her and nodded. "Nice. Confucius. But where is he *now?*"

"He's my partner."

"*Hmmm…*"

"Look, I don't have time to talk ancient history with you—"

"What do you know about four hundred and fifty million

dollars that went missing in his last big case? The serial Killer one." He stepped beside her at the Kia. "Four hundred and fifty...*million...dollars...*"

"I don't know—"

"Cryptocurrency. The keys were stolen from a messenger synthoid working for a law firm."

"I don't know anything about that."

"Maybe you should."

Kim dug in her purse for her keys and thought about Q and his personal MacBook in the Exit Alley conference room.

"It is an awful lot of money And people—different people—are interested in that, too."

"What kind of people?"

"Oh, they can make things happen, too. Bad things."

"I've got to go." She unlocked the doors with her key fob.

"Come on, sis."

"I told you, your way is not *my* way."

"In chaos..."

"Right. *Opportunity.*" Kim opened the door and got in her car. "Go knock somewhere else."

"*Xiao xīn dian.*"

"Drop dead. Okay?"

She closed the door, started her car, and drove off.

Ten blocks away, Kim parked on the street and thought about what her brother told her.

✳✳✳~~~✳✳✳

Monique De La Croix

Monique De La Croix sat alone at a small table set for two in a private room in the Top of the Town restaurant. The windows from the thirty-eighth floor of the Tower at Erieview faced northwest, looking down on the Rock 'n' Roll Hall of Fame, the Science Center, and the Brown's First Energy Stadium. She waited patiently, sipping a Hendrick's Gin martini and gazing west, towards the Gold Coast and the Lake Erie shoreline beyond.

She did not wait long, as the *maître d'* showed Senator Scofield into the room alone and closed the door behind him. Monique stood and turned towards him, taking one last sip of martini before setting her glass down on the table.

The Senator cocked his head slightly to the right. A craggy smile curled his lips upward. *"You…"*

Monique stood herself upright at attention. The fingers of her left hand slid slowly from her collarbone down to the depths between her breasts, while her right hand gently clutched the inside of her thigh and pulled the deep purple hem of her cocktail dress slowly upwards. She flailed her head slowly, throwing her blonde hair across her face.

The Senator took a deep breath.

Monique smiled and stopped just shy of revealing herself. She let her hemline drop and turned, picking up her martini as she stepped over to the window to gaze out on the lake.

The Senator sighed.

She took a long, slow sip of her drink.

He closed his eyes, still smiling.

A gentle knock at the door.

He looked at her one last time, his smile abating. "Yes. Come in."

Their waiter came in and handed the Senator a Manhattan.

"Ms. Del La Croix? Would you care to sit?" the Senator asked.

"Yes. Of course."

The waiter moved quickly to hold her chair out for her. "Another martini, ma'am?"

"Yes, please." She sat, finishing the last of her drink. She gently sucked the olives off of the sword-shaped toothpick and handed the empty glass to the waiter.

The Senator sat down across from her.

"Your usual, sir? The sea bass?" the waiter asked.

"Yes. For both of us. Thank you."

They stared quietly at each other until the waiter brought her drink and left again, closing the door.

"It is very good to…see you again, Monique," the Senator said.

"Of course, it is." She smiled back. "When do you go back to Washington?"

"Late Saturday. After the funeral. I have a committee meeting on Monday."

"And Mrs. Scofield?"

"She will be staying for a while. Family is here and all."

Monique licked her lips slowly.

The Senator lifted his drink to his mouth. He took a deep

breath, held it for four seconds, then exhaled. He drank, then asked, "So, what do we know about the investigation?"

"Well, there were two others who were killed and tattooed with barcodes before Mitchell. And since then a lawyer has also turned up dead."

"Is this the work of a serial killer, then?"

"So it seems."

"Totally random? Nothing to do with A.V. Meridian?"

"Not so far. Though the lawyer, well, he had some…deviant inclinations."

"Don't we all?" The Senator cracked a smile.

"Oh, not like that." Monique frowned back. "It seems he was also tied in with some…dubious characters."

"Ours?"

"Italian. Not the Triad."

"Good. I met with a Lieutenant and some homicide detectives at the station. A man and a Chinese woman."

"Those detectives are actually from the Artificial Crimes Unit. The police believe the attackers are cyberhacked synthoids. They found one of them smashed to the front of a freight train locomotive—well, bits and pieces of it, anyway. What did you tell them?"

"Nothing." The Senator gave Monique a well-practiced look of innocence. "What would I know about any of this?"

"Of course."

"Yes. Of course." The Senator sneered and sipped his Manhattan.

"And the FBI?"

"I made sure they will stand down and let the locals screw it all up."

"Very good." Monique smiled.

The waiter served their sea bass and they ate, trading gossip about fellow members of Congress, their staff, and the Administration.

Monique rested her bare foot between the Senator's legs and gently rubbed his thigh until the waiter returned with coffee.

"When do the shipments begin to arrive?" the Senator asked.

"The first containers are now on the Pacific. Starting in two or three weeks. Some into Los Angeles. Some into the Port of Vancouver."

"Good. Can you stay here and keep an eye on what the police are up to? I do not have anyone else I can trust."

"If you wish. But…" Monique pressed her foot into the Senator's crotch again.

The Senator started to say something but stopped.

Their coffee finished, Monique stood. "I should probably go, then."

The Senator stood, too.

Monique came around the table and gave the Senator a friendly hug.

He buried his nose in her hair and drew in a deep breath.

She gave him a kiss on the cheek, then left without looking back.

In the lobby by the elevator bays, a nondescript synthoid dressed in a dark gray maintenance jumpsuit quietly swept up garbage.

Monique De La Croix ignored him, as usual, when she stepped off elevator number six, but the synthoid acquired her image with CMOS optical sensors. Algorithms automatically calculated her weight at 54.278 kilograms; height at 170.434 centimeters; breasts at 95.834 centimeters; waist at 64.516 centimeters; hips at 87.620 centimeters; and her body mass index at 18.7. Facial recognition software mapped her visage with sixty-eight landmarks.

She breezed past the city street sweeper, dressed in khaki slacks, an oxford shirt, and a tweed jacket, leaning against the wall by the elevators.

He discreetly followed her walk back to the downtown Marriott Hotel.

Shortly after, the maintenance synthoid abandoned his sweeping and shadowed them both.

The Glick Building

"It's creepy, but also kind of clinical." EC shuffled through the pictures taken from Fat Tony's apartment laid out on the pool table in Jake's man cave in the Lakewood Glick Building. "They're too—I don't know, kind of plastic-banana, phony-baloney, you know? The kids don't even look real."

Jake stared at the white-washed wall in front of the sofa pit where he usually projected movies. Now it served as a haphazard recreation of the murder board from Exit Alley with pictures and notes scribbled in Sharpie markers taped to it.

The two-story building was twenty-five feet wide and one hundred feet deep. Jake lived upstairs in the three-bedroom apartment. Downstairs was hollowed out as one big room in the front sixty feet, with a woodworking shop and garage in the back where Jake parked his classic black Ford Mustang convertible and his motorcycles. The front of the building was filled with a plethora of distractions besides the pool table and movie screen wall: a baby grand piano, professional-grade surround sound audio equipment, kayaks stacked on a rack against the east wall, golf clubs, baseball bats, and a well-stocked bar. The exposed brick walls were covered with an eclectic collection of framed artwork, movie posters, and ancient concert handbills for the Beatles, the Allman Brothers, Todd Rundgren, and the Doobie Brothers. Against the back wall was a complete kitchen, which featured a set of glass-fronted refrigerators from his parents' old flower shop, now filled with beer and wine, and a twelve-foot-long oak dining table.

Jake closed his eyes and scratched the back of his head.

"Nothing?" EC asked.

"Zip-zero-nada." Jake came over and leaned on the pool table. He pulled the 10 ball out of the corner pocket, set it on the table between the police department file folders, and spun it. Watching the blue-and-white blur, he asked, "So, how's Wally doing so far?"

"He's doing just fine." EC tossed the pictures of the young boys down on the pool table. "You know, why does the brass always have to screw things up. We were doing good together as partners."

"We're the graybeards, now. We have to share our—" Jake made air quotes with fingers. "—wisdom and experience."

"I did not sign up for any of that. I kind of wanted to just be left alone."

"Ours is not to reason why..."

"Yeah? And so how is Detective Kim working out?"

"Hmm..."

"Yeah. I thought so."

"She's kind of nosy."

"Do I want to know about it?"

Jake exhaled loudly through his mouth. "Probably not."

"Fine with me."

The front door swung open and Wally sauntered into the building. "Hey, there, boys. How are we all doing this fine and wonderful evening?"

Jake and EC watched him walk over to the pool table. He put

his hands on his hips and grinned.

"Detective." Wally winked at EC, then looked at Jake. *"Detec-tive."*

"Okay. Out with it," Jake said.

Wally pulled his notepad out of his jacket pocket and held it up. "I figured it out."

"Oh yeah? What's that?" EC asked.

"The barcodes."

"Seriously?" EC asked.

"Well, I had a little help."

"A little?" Jake asked.

"Well, I was there when it happened. A friend of mine, Amanda—she's a Wiccan—"

"A witch?" asked EC.

"Kind of—I think, but I don't know. It has to do with nature and pagans and gods and goddesses and religion and the third eye…"

"Okay…" Jake squinted at Wally.

"Look, are you interested or not?"

"Sure." Jake shrugged at EC. "Yeah. Go ahead."

Wally flipped the pages of his notebook and laid it down in front of Jake and EC. "Look. It's all right there. Numerology."

There was a knock at the front door.

"Hang on." Jake walked over and pulled back the heavy wooden door.

Kim looked around Jake and saw EC and Wally by the pool table. "What's going on?"

"You know, you're my partner. You don't have to knock every time. Just come on in if it's open."

Kim stepped inside.

"Wally is going to explain the barcodes to us."

"What happened to Q?" Kim asked.

"It's witchcraft, right, Wally?" EC taunted.

"I told you. It's numerology." Wally threw his head back and slapped his hand to his forehead.

"Well, let's have it already," Jake said.

They all leaned on the pool table looking down at Wally's notepad as he explained Chaldean Numerology, the frequencies, and broke down the barcode numbers of each victim based on their names and dates of birth.

"This is kind of wacky," said EC.

"Yeah. But it works." Wally scratched the back of his head. "It's all right there. See?"

Jake walked to the murder board and looked over the victim information beneath the crime scene photos of their dead bodies.

"So, okay…if it is witchcraft, then is there a pattern in the dates of the murders," asked EC. "You know like following a lunar cycle."

"That would be way too easy," Kim said.

"Well, you never know." Wally pulled out his iPhone. "Why don't we just take a look."

"I'm not so sure." Jake shook his head. "I think the sexual angle is key. We've got the chef and the accountant. And they were both clients of Fat Tony."

"Looks like Scofield and Whistler were done pretty close to the full moon. Within a day or two either way." Wally tapped away on his iPhone. "But Burr was killed while there was a new moon. And, of course, Fat Tony was way off—but maybe the killer is accelerating his cycle."

"Or maybe he was just grabbing windows of opportunity for the murders," Kim said.

"I don't know. Seems a little thin." Jake tapped on the picture of Mitchell Scofield lying dead against the dumpster in AsiaTown. "This one seems to be the odd man out, here."

"And we don't really know what's underneath the rocks with the Senator's kid, do we," EC said.

"All we have is the public CV stuff: Yale, then Georgetown, then the company, A.V. Meridian," Kim said. "That's it."

"There's got to be more going on with that kid. A lot more." Jake walked over to the refrigerators, grabbed four Shiner Bock longnecks, and came back to the pool table to pass them out. "What about that woman you met at his apartment? De La Croix?"

"We haven't gone back at her yet," said Wally. "Turns out she really was in Hong Kong the night of the murder, so we don't really have any leverage to push her with."

"She was what? Involved with his business somehow, right?" Kim asked.

"Maddie said she's a Harvard lawyer and listed on the company books as a part-owner. Along with the Senator's brother. Mitchell holds the majority of stock and shares a bank account with his father. They're incorporated in Delaware," Jake popped his beer and took a drink. "She said, the business doesn't stink, but it still doesn't quite smell right either."

"An attorney, huh. Smart, beautiful—and probably rich, too." Wally looked at EC. "Don't you just hate those types?"

"Maybe you and I should talk to her," Jake said to Kim.

"Harvard Law—good luck with that. I hate lawyers," EC muttered. "So, Maddie's helping us?"

"Just checking in to a few items on the DC end of things for us."

"Is that why the Feebs haven't shown up on our doorstep, yet?" Wally asked.

"Unofficially, *though…*"

"What?"

"She mentioned that somebody from the Director's office did come down to talk to her about the case. And me."

"So they know," EC said.

"Well, what about the kid?" Kim asked.

"Seems like the Senator's got things locked down pretty hard about his family. Nobody's talking. And nobody else is asking. Except for Maddie."

"That tells me there's something there," Kim said.

"Damn politicians. I hate them, too," Wally grunted. "But, hey, what about the barcodes? I figured it out, right?"

"Yeah, but what does it mean?" EC asked.

"*Well…*"

"Well, what?" Jake asked.

"I could have Amanda take a closer look at things for us."

"You said she's a witch," EC said.

"It'd be like hiring a psychic to look into things?" Kim asked. "Gee, that sounds just grand."

"It's not so crazy—I mean, her father works in the Security Director's office. Sean. We partnered together in District Four for a while. A long time ago." Wally looked warily at Kim. "Anyway, if I let her have some background info on the vics, she can, well, do her thing."

"Her thing?" Jake asked.

Wally sighed and shook his head. "The frequencies—the

numbers have to be interpreted, you know, with details about them and, maybe, some astrology…and, ah, like tarot card readings…and a bunch of other stuff. I don't know everything."

"Hey, why not," Jake said. "She cracked the barcodes while we were all scratching our heads. Maybe she can get us some insight on the perp and what he's thinking."

"Okay. Great." Wally finished off his beer.

"The kid's funeral, when is it?" Jake asked.

"Saturday," EC said.

"Where's it at?"

"St. John's, downtown."

"Maybe we need eyes on the church crowd and the cemetery," Jake said. "To see who all shows up…and who doesn't. You and Wally take the church. Kim and I will watch the cemetery."

"Figures you'd bail on getting caught inside a house of God," EC said. "Okay. I'm out of here."

"Yeah. Me, too," said Wally.

Jake watched Wally leave out the front door and EC head towards the back. Jake leaned down at the end of the pool table. He looked at Kim. "So, what brings you by tonight?"

Kim sipped her half-empty Shiner Bock. "I just wanted to talk about the case some."

Jake spun the 10 ball again and watched the blur.

"So, if Wally figured out the barcodes, what about Q?"

"Q?"

"What's he going to do on the case now?"

"Well, we'll have him check the numerology thing out, too. Just to be sure. And I asked him to dig around in some online chat rooms to try to chase down Fat Tony's activities."

"Oh…"

"Anything else?"

Kim shook her head. "No. I don't think so."

"Good."

"Yeah…I guess I'll go, too." She left the rest of her beer on the edge of the pool table and headed towards the front door.

Jake spun the 10 ball again and watched her leave.

~~~

Mechanical

Jake walked into the Mechanical Department and over to the work table where Puff sat on a tall stool examining synthoid cranial modules meticulously laid out in front of him. The empty Dermaloy skin lay wrinkled on the far left. The white carbon fiber skull was split and set next to it, with pairs of aural, optical, and olfactory sensors laid out in a hollowed-out face form. The tangled wires of the jawbone's nanomotors and micro hydraulic wave actuators for lip, tongue, and facial expressions were below it with the linear motor tone generator. To the far right, black-box modules, printed circuit boards, and flex circuits were arranged in an orderly grid.

"What do you want?" Puff growled through his gritted teeth, holding a flex circuit chipset within an inch of his eyeballs, as he tried to read the serial number.

"This our ANSUB?"

"What's left of him. Not much to tell, since all we got was his noggin. Definitely Gen 1. Definitely long past its expiration date. Other than that…"

Jake looked around. "Where's Bob?"

"He's on a donut run. There won't be enough for you, too. So don't even think about it, pal."

"Eh, no worries."

Puff set the flex circuit back down in its place in the grid.

He stared straight ahead. "Where's *your* partner?"

"Back in the Alley, I guess."

Puff spun on his stool to look at Jake. He crossed his arms over his chest. He looked up at the ceiling, then back directly at Jake. "She is wound tighter than bark on a tree. What's up with that?"

Jake realized there was no sense in trying to fake it with Puff. "Complications."

"*Complications?* I hate complications."

"Yeah, me, too."

"Well, what are you going to do about it? I don't want complications in my shop."

"I do not know…"

"Maybe she needs to get the carbon blown off her head gaskets to get herself into a better disposition."

"Hey, Jake," Bob said as he came into the shop, carrying a box of donuts. "Where's Kim? Huh?"

"We were just discussing his partner," said Puff.

"You know, she's cuter than a speckled pup."

"Cute?" Jake searched Puff's face for an explanation.

"See what I have to put up with? Dammit," Puff said. "So, what are you going to do about it?"

"Are you and her having…*issues?*" Bob asked.

"I didn't come in here for couples counseling. Let's just talk about the droid."

Bob put his hand on Jake's shoulders. He leaned in to half-whisper in his ear, "Is it professional? Or personal?"

Puff gave Jake a squinty-eyed look.

"Look, she comes with baggage. Things went sideways between her and some guys in Narcotics."

"Yeah, I heard something about that." Bob winked at Jake. "You know, we do hear things down here."

"What? What's that?" Puff asked.

"She got squeezed between some bad cops and Internal Affairs. I think some of them went to jail. Right?" Bob asked Jake.

"What about her?" Puff asked.

"She ended up in Artificial Crimes…with me."

"You know what I mean. Did she squeal?" asked Puff.

Jake shrugged his shoulders. "Her brother carries a shield in IA."

"So, what are you doing wrong, then?" Puff pointed his finger at Jake.

"Me?"

"You don't trust her, do you?" Puff asked.

"Trust?"

"Yeah. That's bad news in a partner." Puff pointed at Bob. "He annoys the hell out of me, but I trust him."

"You know, Jake, you shouldn't jump to conclusions. See what I have to put up with every day?" Bob waved his hand at Puff and shook his head. "Maybe you need to, you know, sit down and have a beer together—or maybe a glass of wine—and talk things out. *Like adults.*"

"Huh. Interesting. So if she really is working with Internal Affairs, this former undercover cop wouldn't have any problem lying to me about it."

"I didn't think about that." Bob asked Puff, "Did you?"

"I don't want to think about any of this stuff. I've got my hands full with that guy there." Puff pointed at Bob, then turned around and picked up a one-inch by two-inch double-layered circuit board to examine. "Just let me do my work."

"Hey, you were the one that asked me. Remember?" Jake said.

"Didn't you work undercover, too?" Bob asked.

The door to Mechanical opened and closed. Puff looked over his shoulder.

"Jake. Are you here? EC said to check." Kim walked over. She looked from Jake to Bob to Puff, then back at Jake and frowned. "What?"

"Ah…Do you want a donut?" Bob held out the box.

Onion Sites

For the fourth night in a row, Q cruised slowly and silently through a residential neighborhood, this time near Kamm's Corner at 1:30 in the morning in his Tesla Model S. He checked the WiFi scanner output running on a burner version of a Windows laptop. He slowed, crawled a bit forward, then back, and parked on the street. He killed his lights. It didn't take long to hack into the SSID. He fired up his VPN, selecting a server, this time based in Budapest, Hungary. He started his Tor browser and logged on to an I2P Reseed Server to safely and anonymously surf the Darknet.

Q had created hundreds of online IDs to move in and out of different unlisted .onion websites without leaving a trace, nor any breadcrumb links to other sites. Most of the IDs were lurkers, which allowed him to anonymously cruise the discussion forums and chat rooms. Others he used to return and make posts to engage users directly, with cautiously worded questions or camouflaged comments to draw out more information without revealing his investigatory intent.

On his first night out, the depravity expressed on the Hard Candy child pornography websites was stunning and horrifying. By now his mind had become numb to it. He told himself that half of it must be the expressions of the delusional fantasies of seriously disturbed individuals, and tried very hard to ignore the other half. He adopted a clinical attitude as he scoured the discussion forum histories at 3DBoys, 7axxn, Axel's Blue Zone, and others, looking for any signs of Fat Tony, Alan Burr, Paul Whistler, or Mitchell Scofield. It was a small, depressing world, yet he found few clues.

His patience wore down to near zero around 3:30, reading pathetic, twisted screeds about the need to "enlighten kids" and to help the rest of the world see that so-called "children" are human beings who enjoy sexuality as much as "adults."

Q set aside his laptop.

He closed his eyes and breathed deep, held his breath for four seconds, then exhaled and waited four more seconds.

He did it again and then again.

"Dammit!" Q shook his head. "Numerology…"

Why didn't I think of that?

Wally's friend, Amanda, was right about the Chaldean numerology connection in the barcodes.

But, still, what did it mean?

Q grabbed the laptop and searched the Darknet on "witchcraft," which resulted in several Hard Candy websites with photos of even more perverted satanic rituals involving obviously illegal sex, but no evidence of Fat Tony or the others. He studied the scene settings looking for symbols and signs, but there were few besides the usual pentacles and triple moons.

Searching the surface web again for witchcraft symbols, Q found those and the other typical signs of Earth, Air, Water, Fire, the Triquetra, the Horn Triskelion, and others.

He paused to think, then went to the website www.avmeridian.com—and there it was: their corporate logo was a version of the Horn Triskelion, otherwise known as the Triple Horn of Odin.

Q returned to the page of witchcraft symbols to learn that

the Horn Triskelion represents wisdom, cleverness, communication, and is used to represent both female and male energies on an altar…

He closed his eyes and recalled the discussion forum postings about the need for pedophiles to "enlighten kids" and to "help the rest of the world see" that so-called children are human beings who enjoy sexuality.

Wisdom…

Communication…

"Those sons of bitches…" Q muttered out loud.

~~~

Cathedral of St. John the Evangelist

Wally sat in the last pew, leaning sideways against the back, watching the entrance as Cathedral of St. John slowly filled for the funeral of Mitchell Scofield.

His notepad sat on his lap. He kept a tally at the top and listed the occasional celebrity—politicians, TV anchors, radio show hosts, businessmen—neatly below. He mainly watched for the odd men out, the loners who skirted the edges and did not seem to recognize or acknowledge the others, but there were few. He noted their heights, weights, builds, hair color, facial features, and dress. Conveniently, most of them sat scattered around Wally in the back of the church.

Between times, Wally carefully studied the stained-glass windows of The Nativity, Jesus in the Temple, The Last Supper, and The Ascension. He noted the craftsmanship of the carved marble columns supporting the arching ceiling above, the shrines along the walls, the Appalachian oak carvings behind the altar, the life-sized crucifix above the south entrance, and, finally, the casket in front of the sanctuary.

The crowd flowed into the pews, spilling back towards the entrance, mostly older couples and some families. Wally slouched down and away when the Safety Director entered with his uniformed entourage of District Captains. He did not escape the scowling eye, though, of Amanda's father, Sean.

At five minutes before two, the Senator and his wife slowly walked up the aisle followed by Mitchell's two brothers and sister with their wives, husband, and children. The Senator's brother came behind with his family.

Wally watched the Senator adroitly work the crowd on his way to their pew in front—squeezing a shoulder here and there, grasping a woman's hand, a quick, but firm handshake, pausing to accept condolences or leaning down to whisper in an ear.

The Senator let his wife into the pew in front of the pulpit. He looked back over the crowd seated behind them as if searching for someone in particular, then sat beside her. He noticed his wife staring at Mitchell's casket. He dutifully took her hand.

His family filled in behind him.

As soon as the Senator and his family were seated, the Bishop, priests, and altar boys came in and took their places.

EC came around the far side and slid Wally over in the pew. He had been standing on the south side of Superior Avenue watching from the outside.

"Anything?" he asked.

"A few here and there," Wally whispered back. He nodded towards a couple of the lone wolves.

The priest began the ceremony.

"What about her?"

"Her, who?"

"Monique De La Croix."

Wally looked at EC. "That's strange. I didn't see her."

"Yeah…neither did I."

Lake View Cemetery

Kim and Jake were positioned on a rise above the gravesite for Mitchell Scofield, behind a large, square family tombstone for Mr. and Mrs. Wilson Walker. A pair of binoculars and a camera with a 70-300mm telephoto lens sat on top.

Kim propped herself on the tombstone and examined the burial site through a second set of binoculars.

"Anything, yet?" Jake asked. He leaned against an oak tree gazing at the misty horizon over Lake Erie.

"All quiet." She set the binoculars down and cast her eyes at Jake. "You think we'll learn anything?"

"Eh…doubtful. But you have to run out every grounder."

"And you didn't want to go to the church?"

"Not so much."

Kim took a deep breath, then exhaled.

Jake looked over.

"You know, you never asked," Kim said. "And we're partners now."

Jake turned back towards the lake. An oar boat churned towards Detroit five miles out. "I assumed you're like me."

"Like you?"

"I figured you're a good cop. You got sideways and they didn't know what else to do with you. So, they sent you to the Geek Squad."

"I am a good cop."

Jake nodded. "So, I was right."

Kim took a breath but held her thoughts.

"I don't need to know the gory details unless you feel the need to get them off your chest."

Kim shook her head.

"Yeah. It doesn't really matter, I guess," Jake said.

"But it does. I was right."

"Me, too. And now you're here with me." Jake walked over to the tombstone and leaned on it. "Some salvation, eh?"

"At least I'm working a case."

"There you go." Jake winked at her. "It's all there is for us types."

Kim closed her eyes. "You know…"

Jake looked down at Mitchell Scofield's gravesite. "What?"

"My brother works for Internal Affairs."

"That's his tough luck. I don't track their roster."

"He asked me about four hundred and fifty million dollars."

Jake picked up his binoculars, holding them to his eyes. "Yeah…Q's been looking for it and found it in a crypto account in the Cayman Islands. But you knew that already, right?"

"Yeah. I *detected* something like that."

"Can't pull the wool over your eyes."

Jake peered through the binoculars.

Kim studied the tops of her shoes. "Jake, this is just you and me talking here. I'm, ah, not wired."

"Why would you be? You didn't rat those other guys out. I know that."

"How?"

"I just do. What other choice did you have?"

"You trust me?"

Jake set the binoculars down and stepped over close to Kim. He smiled. "That's not something you get for free. You earn it."

"And?"

"So far, so good…*I guess.*" Jake cocked his head and squinted at Kim. "So…what brought your brother around to see you?"

"He is such an…*ass-hat.*"

Jake laughed. "You have to love family. He wants you to work for them, huh?"

"He knows I'm not happy here."

"Who is? But when you shoot a councilman's son…"

"You were cleared, though."

"And he deserved it." Jake leaned on the tombstone. "But his father was a councilman. So it was this or being a private investigator."

"Not your style?"

Jake shook his head. "I don't want to work for a living—chasing down cases. Too much marketing."

"So, what about the four hundred and fifty million? Is Q trying to get it back?"

"Well, here's the interesting thing. We thought for sure the Baron pulled that heist off."

"And he's dead, right?"

"Right, but there's been some movement on the Bitcoins." Jake looked down on the gravesite, noticing a hearse trailed by several limos and a line of expensive sedans with their headlights on pull up. "Looks like the party's arrived."

Kim looked down. "What movement?"

"About a hundred grand of payouts." Jake picked up the camera and sighted on the open hole in the ground. He started taking pictures of the mourners as they got out of their cars.

"Who's doing that?"

"That, my detective friend, is a very good question."

~~

The Meat Locker

She woke up naked, chained by her ankle to the bed frame, her head throbbing. A twenty-five-watt bare light bulb hung from the ceiling casting dim shadows on the inside of the meat refrigerator through the empty hooks hanging from rollers.

Monique De La Croix screamed as loud as she could.

Outside, sitting at the workbench, the street cleaner paused, hearing her muffled cry. He looked over at the heavy, six-inch-thick insulated wooden door and smiled.

No one will ever hear her.

He went back to sorting synthoid parts.

Iris & Dolly's Bistro

Q stopped at the front door to Iris & Dolly's Bistro on West 25th Street in Ohio City. He asked Jake, "You ever been here before?"

"No. I haven't." Jake looked at Kim. "You?"

She shook her head.

Q said, "It's Paul Whistler's place."

"Yeah. I recognize it from the pictures of his food truck at the murder scene," Jake said.

"And you know about Iris and Dolly, right?" Q asked. *"Taxi Driver and Lolita."*

"Jodie Foster and…ah…" Kim frowned at Jake.

"Dominique Swain," Jake said.

"You get the picture then, right?" Q pushed in the door and held it open for them. "Do you like art?"

Kim furrowed her brow to give Q a curious look as she passed by.

Jake gave a half-smile.

"You'll see."

The interior of the dining room had the dim look of a moonlit night, even in the middle of the afternoon. They waited at the hostess podium until a very young-looking, auburn-haired woman waved them in. "Sit anywhere you like. I'll be with you in a minute."

"Shouldn't you be in school?" Jake teased.

She winked back at him.

There were a couple of middle-aged men sitting alone nursing their drinks at the bar, who ignored them. At the far end, a cook worked on a grocery list.

Kim and Q claimed a table in the middle of the bistro, where they could see the entire room.

Jake wandered by and went down a long hall along the side of the kitchen. He pushed open the rear exit door, squinting in the sunlight, and noticed Whistler's food truck in the back parking lot, released from the impound lot. The door swung shut and Jake checked the men's room, then went into the lady's room without knocking on the way back to the table. It was empty, too. He sat down so he could see both the front and the back doors to either side. His eyes slowly adjusted to the dim lighting.

"Hey, guys. What will you have?" the waitress asked, coming up to the table. She laid out round cardboard coasters in front of each of them with the Horn Triskelion symbol on the top. The three interwoven horns were entwined with serpent heads. Around the outside, Iris & Dolly's Bistro was imprinted top and bottom in an ancient Greek font face.

No one else noticed, except Q. He smiled.

Jake looked over at the beer bottles above the bar. "I'll have a Smithwick's." He looked at Kim. "What?"

"On duty?"

"Just blending in."

"I'll have a glass of Merlot." Kim stuck her tongue out at Jake.

Jake smiled and looked around at the paintings and framed photos on the walls. There were a few prominently displayed black-and-white shots of Jodie Foster in short-shorts and a tank top and Dominique Swain close-ups with milk on her upper lip

Motherless Children

from *Taxi Driver and Lolita.* A shadowed silhouette of a man in charcoal was posted near the front. In the back was the drawing of an undressed teenage boy. Nearly naked young girls in bathing suits kneeling in a locker room shower looking back over their shoulders with their hands hiding their asses. A five-pointed star crudely drawn over the navel of a woman. Large, framed posters of Led Zeppelin's *Houses of the Holy* and Nirvana's *Nevermind* album covers with naked children. Two men standing with knives and forks over a naked man lying on a round dinner table, evidently ready to eat.

"Ice tea," said Q. He picked up his coaster and spun it around between his thumb and his middle finger. When the waitress left, he held it out for Kim and Jake to see. "Know what this is?"

Kim shook her head. "No. What?"

Q caught Jake's visual distraction and sat back for a moment.

Kim noticed, too. She began to look around at the art on the walls. "Yikes!"

Over their heads, Jake noticed the life-sized headless silver and bronze castings hanging by wires from the ceiling of naked men and women contorted in sexually suggestive arches and poses.

The waitress returned with their drinks. "Did you want to order lunch?"

"Give us a minute or two, okay?" Q said.

"Whistler certainly has a theme going on here," muttered Jake.

"Jake."

"What?"

Q held up the coaster. "Here's your connection."

"What's that?"

"The triple horn of Odin." Q passed the coaster to Jake. "Originally, he was a Norse god."

"Yeah…and?"

Q brought up the A.V. Meridian website on his phone. He pointed it at Jake. "And here. Check out their logo."

"Nearly the same," said Kim.

"What's that mean?" Jake asked.

"Do you really want to know?" Q asked.

"That's why you brought us here, isn't it?"

Q smirked. "Yeah, I guess so. I think these guys hijacked the symbol from the witches."

"What guys?" Jake asked.

"The pedos. Remember, you asked me to look into this stuff. Kind of like the white supremacist guys took over the Solar Cross for their crazy nationalistic schemes." Q looked at Jake, then at Kim. He held up the coaster and his iPhone again. "Look they're the same."

"So, what does it mean?" Kim asked.

"What was Whistler arrested for?"

"He got caught with a young field hockey player from Magnificat," Jake said. "And Fat Tony made it all go away."

"And you don't think that was just an accident, right? Look at this place. Look at the artwork. Look at the pictures of Jody Foster and Dominique Swain."

"Yeah…this was no boating accident." Jake surveyed the room again.

"The Horn Triskelion represents wisdom, cleverness, communication. It is also used to represent both female and male energies on an altar…" Q tapped on the Triskelion logos on the screen of A.V. Meridian's website. "It's a symbol of their way of…*normalizing* what they believe."

"Kids, right?" Kim asked.

Q nodded.

She shook her head. "And Mitchell Scofield?"

"It is *his* company."

"And the Senator?" Jake asked.

Q shrugged his shoulders. "Those guys, they're all control freaks. That's how they hold onto their power for years and years and years. Nothing gets by them."

Jake grimaced. He stared at the painting of two men with knives and forks standing over the naked man on the table.

"Then who's killing them all?" Kim asked.

"Hey, you guys are the detectives." Q smiled and took a sip of iced tea.

"Do you want to eat here?" Jake asked Kim.

"Not really."

"Yeah, me neither." Jake reached into his back pocket and pulled out his wallet. He dropped two twenties on the table. "Come on. Let's get out of here."

~~~

The Marriott at Key Center

"This is the room, sir," said the tall, thin Marriott Assistant Manager for Security. He stepped back from the door. He stood at ease near the opposite wall.

"Thanks," Wally said.

EC pointed at the "Do Not Disturb" sign hanging from the doorknob. "When was the last time the room was cleaned?"

"One moment please." The Assistant Manager reached inside his suit jacket to use his radio to call housekeeping. He listened on his headset. "Looks, like four days ago."

Wally pounded on the door with his fist and called out loudly, "Ms. De La Croix!"

They listened but heard nothing.

"And no one's seen her in the hotel?"

The Assistant Manager shook his head. "Not that I know of."

"Ms. De La Croix!" Wally knocked hard again. He looked at EC. "What do you think?"

EC took a deep breath and pulled out his Glock. "Can I have the key? And I need you to wait down the hall...there, please."

The Assistant Manager nodded and stepped back.

"Me?" Wally asked.

"Yeah, you first."

Wally sighed and drew his pistol.

EC unlocked the door and Wally quickly moved inside the suite.

EC followed behind him.

Wally cleared to the left.

EC cleared right.

The front room of the suite was empty. Wally moved to check the corner bedroom. EC went through and checked the bathroom. Both were cleared quickly. They holstered their pistols.

Wally stared at the made-up bed. "What are the chances she's been making her own bed and cleaning up the joint?"

"Yeah, I don't see it." EC gazed intently around the room. "Why don't you go take care of the Marriott guy and I'll look around."

Wally went out and EC began pulling open the dresser drawers, which were filled with neatly folded women's clothes. Dress and pants suits hung with blouses in the closet. The bathtub and sink were extremely dry. The mirrors were clean. Her toiletries and lotion bottles were carefully lined up on the sink counter. The soaps were dry.

In the front room of the suite, EC opened De La Croix's laptop on the desk and clicked the power button. He shuffled through manila folders in her briefcase: one for expenses, one filled with documents written in Chinese; and one labeled Pac-Cyber Limited, which contained two sets of shipping paperwork, including Shipping Quotes, Commercial Invoices, Certificates of Origin. Material Safety Data Sheets, Shipper's Letters of Instruction, Booking Confirmations, Bills of Lading, Packing Lists, and Letters of Credit. According to the Bills of Lading, it appeared two twenty-foot, Full Container Loads were en route. One scheduled to arrive in Los Angeles in fifteen days and the second coming into the Port of Vancouver in thirty-two days. EC used his phone to take photos of all the documents.

The laptop booted but was password-protected, so he shut it down. He tried to open the safe, but it was locked. There was little more to go on.

Wally stepped back out into the hall. "So, is this a decent gig or what?"

"Not bad. But not really much action—if you know what I mean."

Wally read the name tag on the Assistant Manager's jacket. "So, John, how'd you end up here?"

"I landed this gig after I got out of the Army. I was an MP."

"But, it's not what you want, though, right?" Wally stared him down.

"Oh, hell no. I'm working on a BA in Criminology at Cleveland State. You gotta love the G.I. Bill."

"Yeah, you do."

"What about you?"

"I was a mud-eater in the Marines. So what's up after school? Cleveland PD?"

"Well, actually, I'd rather go with the Feds. You know, in the DOJ somewhere—wherever they'll take me. I don't really care. You can't beat the benefits."

"Cool."

EC came out of the room. "What's going on out here?"

"Well, John, here, doesn't really have any info on Ms. De La Croix, but he'll take us down to the front desk to talk to them."

"Let's do it," said EC.

The Assistant Manager led them to the elevator and took them into the office behind the counter. Wally questioned the desk clerks and the Concierge. No one had seen Ms. De La Croix for three days.

"What kind of charges did she have against the room?" EC asked.

The head clerk hesitated, waiting on the Assistant Manager.

"She's been missing, what three days?" John asked Wally.

"Something like that," Wally said. "We're just trying to make sure she's okay."

"It's okay," John told her.

They followed the clerk out to the front desk, then she logged into the computer. "Ms. De La Croix has had several charges at the lobby bar and a massage at the spa. She had the massage six days ago. There are a couple of room services charges and some lobby bar charges. The last one was Wednesday in the bar at twelve-fifteen."

EC peered over her shoulder and wrote the information in his notepad. "That was five days ago."

"And nothing else has been added to her tab since?" Wally asked.

The desk clerk shook her head.

"The funeral was Saturday," Wally said to EC, "which means she went missing last Thursday or Friday."

"Looks like Jake was right," EC said. "We'll have to get a BOLO out on her when we get back."

~~~

The Mainstream Media

Kim paused on her way to the police parking lot when she noticed Kristie from *Five Alive News* standing next to her car staring at her iPhone, scrolling through screen after screen. She looked around and did not see a cameraman. She waited and watched for a few minutes, then walked slowly to her car.

Kristie was absorbed by her phone.

So Kim hit the lock button on her key fob, setting off the horn.

Kristie eyes slowly rose up from her phone. She smiled as Kim approached. "Detective. So nice to see you again."

Kim hit the key fob again to unlock her car.

Kristie stepped between Kim and the front door. "So, where is Jake?"

"You don't know?"

"I don't keep him on a leash. He's free to come and go as he pleases."

Kim smiled. "How nice for him. He left about a half-hour ago. Is there something I can do for you, then?"

"Perhaps…perhaps…" Kristie smiled back. "You know, I'm awfully thirsty. Damn near parched."

"Yeah, I don't know about that—"

"You're off duty right? What's the harm?" Kristie gave Kim a sly, sideways look. "Come on. It'll be fun. Just us girls."

"Just us girls?"

"That's okay. I get it. Don't want to get caught sleeping with the enemy."

"Ah, that would be you and Jake."

"Oh…yeah…so it is."

"So, what is that whole thing all about anyway?"

"He's really just a big kid. Likes to play cops and robbers—and he's pretty damn good at it."

"What does that have to do with—"

"Oh, Kim…" Kristie shook her head. "You know, his girlfriend, Amy, got thrown off the Main Avenue Bridge and killed the night he finally caught up with the Baron. That was pretty ugly. And, of course, shortly after that Maddie joined the FBI and moved to Washington D.C. without telling him she was pregnant with Wyatt."

"So you feel sorry for him?"

"Never let a crisis go to waste." Kristie made a half-fist and examined her finely polished fingernails. "And there are definitely benefits for *moi*. If you know what I mean."

"I definitely don't need to hear this." Kim put her hand over her eyes.

"You know, the gene pool's a little thin for someone in my business. A phony-baloney news anchor? A lying politician? A mind-numbed athlete? Or maybe just an old, boring college professor?"

Kim looked up at Kristie. "Really? What about, *sleeping with the enemy?*"

"That's the thing about spies. Most of the secrets we keep are from each other." Kristie winked at Kim. "It's kind of fun."

"I think I need to get going."

"So, no drinkypoo?"

Kim stepped around Kristie and reached for the door handle.

"No? Okay, then…just one more thing."

Kim opened the door and turned back. *"What?"*

"Why are you hiding information about the missing four-hundred-fifty million dollars?"

"Oh, God, *my brother!*" Kim blurted out.

"You mean, Rick? In Internal Affairs?" Kristie displayed her perfect white teeth in a smile. "I don't reveal my sources."

Kim quickly got in her car, backed up, and squealed her tires pulling out of the parking lot.

Kristie had stepped back to watch, then scrolled through the screens on her phone again.

~~~

Battery Park

Thursday evening, Robbie Bennington stepped out of his Battery Park townhome and headed on foot towards the pedestrian connection at the end of West 76th Street to Edgewater Park. He took a long pull off a newly opened Corona.

The music had already started from the RTA Main Stage at the Edgewater Beach House.

He turned and shuffled down the long, sloping ramp, entering the narrow opening leading under the railroad tracks. Dim yellow lights along the top of the west wall glowed in the twilight near the bend in the middle of the tunnel.

Robbie slowed his steps at the turn when he noticed the silhouette of a woman leaning back against the concrete wall halfway to the exit. Her head was nodding towards her chest.

Was she crying? No, but…

He sauntered forward. He grinned.

But what does it matter?

Robbie took a brief pull off the clear longneck bottle, squinting one eye shut as he took in her young figure down its length. He did not recognize her, as he nonchalantly shuffled her way.

The nodding slowed and stopped, head still down.

He paused beside her. "Are you heading down to the Beach…"

Looking up, he was arrested by the cold blue eyes—the left hand grabbed his neck, effortlessly lifted him up, and slammed him around hard against the concrete wall.

Robbie dropped his beer bottle and it broke. Gagging, he clenched at the hand as it effortlessly squeezed his carotid arteries off.

He rasped weakly. The grey closed in on his peripheral vision as he locked on the unblinking, cold blue eyes.

It squeezed his neck hard against the wall.

Robbie's lungs sucked for air. He grasped at his neck with his fingers and thrashed his legs wildly, inside hearing the crush of his cricoid cartilage as he lost consciousness.

The hand squeezed harder.

Robbie went limp. The spasm in his diaphragm strained to draw in a breath.

It squeezed ever more tightly around the sides of his neck, pushing him against the wall until the ribbon-mounted piezoresistive silicon pressure sensors in the fingers could no longer feel blood pumping against its grip in the carotid arteries.

It dropped him into a heap on the ground. CMOS sensors zoomed in and captured the image of his lifeless eyes gazing into space. It kicked him over to laser a barcode on the small of his back, then captured its image.

Calmly stepping over Robbie, it made the turn in the tunnel and escaped into Battery Park.

~~~

The microwave completed its countdown and beeped at the same time his computer pinged and thumbnails of Robbie's dead face and barcode appeared at the top of his screen.

He clicked on Robbie's portrait to open the png file. Grabbing a red Sharpie, he went to the wall in the butcher shop and slowly X-ed out his mugshot. He smiled a bit as he maliciously colored in his eyes as well.

The photos were transferred to a solid-state drive, then he checked the meatloaf dinner in the microwave. He started it again for two minutes.

As it cooked, he went to the meat locker door and looked through the small window at his captive.

Monique De La Croix sat pressing herself into the far corner at the head of the bed. Her forehead rested against her knees.

It had been such a foolish impulse, he thought. *But…*

Monique raised her head. She looked over at the door with pure hatred in her eyes.

He instinctively stepped back.

The microwave stopped and beeped again.

He sighed, took his meatloaf to the workbench, and slowly ate his dinner.

~~~

The Rede

"What is it you're not telling me?" Amanda demanded of Wally.

He browsed around the Moonglow shop, meandering about, picking up items off the shelves, pretending to closely examine them, then setting them back down again. "Yeah, your dad said to come see you."

She stood behind the counter and watched him carefully.

Wally came to a collection of silver necklaces hanging from an improvised driftwood display. He flipped through the pendants of Ankhs, Celtic Shield Knots, Triskeles, and Triquetras, until he came to the Triple Horn of Odin. He picked it off the display and brought it close to his eyes to examine.

"That is—"

"The Triple Horn."

"—*of Odin.*"

Wally nodded, then looked over at Amanda. He walked over to the counter and set it down. "How much?"

She picked it up, dangling it from her fingers. "Eighty-five dollars."

"Okay." Wally reached for his wallet.

"Just take it." She held it out towards him.

Wally stared down at her.

"Just tell me why."

Wally leaned down on the counter, He looked at the Triple

Horn, then at Amanda. "It's about the case."

"And?"

"I should really pay you for this."

"*Wally!*" She stamped her foot down.

He nodded slowly. He smiled. "That's what I like about you."

"*What is it you're not telling me?*"

"These people—you know, the victims. They are not such nice people."

"I know how to use a computer. I know how to search the web," Amanda said. "I know they were…involved in certain…unsavory things."

"*Unsavory?*"

"That's what my dad said. Unsavory."

Wally nodded.

"And he wanted to know why I was involved."

"And you told your dad how you solved the whole barcode thing, right?"

"So, what does this mean?" She held up the Triple Horn.

"I just want you to know that I—I'm getting this all second, or third hand. I'm not into any of that stuff—at all."

"What stuff?"

"Jake asked Q to look into—to go into the Darknet and dig around in some of its blacker corners."

"Like what?"

"Well, Paul Whistler has a bistro in Ohio City. It's called Iris & Dolly's. Do you know about that place?"

Amanda shook her head.

"Do you know who Iris and Dolly are? They're characters—young girls—very young girls—from the book *Lolita* and the movie *Taxi Driver.*"

"You mean like…"

"Like twelve years old. Iris was a prostitute. And Dolly was really Lolita who becomes…involved—sexually with her stepfather."

"Ugh!" Amanda stepped back from the counter.

"Yeah, and it seems Whistler got nabbed with an underaged girl. Like fourteen, I think. And the attorney, Anthony Eliot, got him off scot-free."

"How could he? He's a lawyer."

"A lawyer?" Wally ground out a grim laugh between his clenched teeth. "Well, besides his barcode, Fat Tony also had an *unsavory* tattoo about young boys. And you don't want to know what we found in his apartment."

"People are not supposed to do that. It's not the way."

"The way?"

"An' ye harm none, do what ye will." Amanda pointed her finger at Wally. *"Harm none!"*

Wally took a deep breath and exhaled. "Yeah…"

"This is not witchcraft."

"No, but…" Wally dug his phone out of his pants pocket. He pulled up a photo and held it out for Amanda. "Look familiar?"

Amanda nodded. She looked at the Triple Horn necklace, then back at the picture on the screen. She shook her head. "No…*no…*"

"That's a coaster from Whistler's bistro."

Amanda dropped the necklace to the counter. She pushed it away, towards Wally, and crossed her arms over her chest. "So is somebody killing these people because they are witches or because they are pedophiles?"

"Q thinks the pervs have hijacked the Triple Horn symbol.

Like how the Nazis started using the Solar Cross. He says it's because the Triple Horn stands for wisdom and cleverness and communication. That these guys feel like they're so much smarter and enlightened than the rest of us normies and they need to *teach* us all about…" Wally picked up the necklace and looked at it. "It's sick, isn't it?"

"That's not what we're all about. That's not who we are."

"Yeah, I know. I know. But maybe the killer doesn't know that."

"And is that why he's marking them with numerology barcodes?"

Wally shrugged his shoulders. "I don't know. Maybe."

"And the Senator's son, too?"

Wally navigated to the homepage for A.V. Meridian on his phone and held it out towards Amanda, showing her the company logo. "A.V. Meridian is Mitchell Scofield's company."

"That's the Triple Horn, too."

Wally nodded.

"But his father…"

"Yeah…*his father.*"

~~~

Li Wah

Jake walked into the Li Wah Restaurant in AsiaTown. He knew exactly which table to go to, back by the fish tanks.

Jake looked down at Jhing Xho, then glanced up over his shoulders at the tilapia floating in the aquariums. He noticed roast ducks hanging from hooks behind the glass in the display case. "You rang?"

"So good of you to join me." Jhing Xho waved at the chair across from him. "Please, sit."

Jake noticed the ever-present bodyguards in a nearby booth watching closely.

"Some tea?" Jhing Xho held up the teapot.

"No Frappuccino?"

"It is traditional."

"Sure. Why not." Jake sat down.

Jhing Xho filled his cup. He smiled.

Jake returned the grin. "Did you order?"

"No, no, no. I was waiting for you to arrive." He waved his arm abruptly to signal their waiter, who came right over. He gave a lengthy order in Chinese, then noticed Jake staring at the aquariums again. "Or would you prefer, rather, lobster…or, perhaps, the crab?"

"No, you're doing great. You're doing just fine."

Jhing Xho nodded and completed his order.

The waiter bowed slightly and scurried off to the kitchen.

"Now, Jake, your friend—the young one."

"Q?"

"What kind of name is that anyway? Is it like the movies? Like James Bond?"

"Yeah. It is."

Jhing Xho shook his head in wonder. "I know he has found our money."

"Your money?"

"Oh, no. It is not all my money. It is more like a syndicate's money."

"What syndicate?"

"Really, it is of little importance to you right now."

"Yeah…I don't think so." Jake leaned in on his elbows. "I am intensely curious, now."

Jhing Xho rolled his fingers impatiently on the table. "Now, Jake…I just ordered our delicious dinner. Are we going to have a friendly conversation or will we be forced to eat in silence? I do not think that is good for our digestion."

"Okay. We'll come back to the syndicate."

"Thank you. Of course, my friends are most interested in seeing this money returned. We hold no ill intents towards any…innocent adventures."

"How did you find out about Q?"

"Oh, Jake. We are Asian. Have you not seen our SAT scores? Very, very high in mathematics."

Jake smiled. "Granted. But Q is pretty smart, too."

"Yes. Indeed. Indeed, he is."

"And you know there is an issue here. I mean, somebody's been spending this money—you know that, right?"

"This has not been Mr. Q?"

Jake shook his head.

"Oh, dear." Jhing Xho rubbed his chin. "Who, then?"

"Hmmm…a real Charlie Chan-type mystery, huh?"

Jhing Xho grimaced. "You should not make fun of this situation."

"Nor should you." Jake sipped his tea. "So, why was *the syndicate* giving this money to Stein, Baylor, and Stein?"

"It was an investment."

"An investment in what, pray tell?"

"You are going to make me have this conversation."

Jake nodded.

"Well…" Jhing Xho sat back as their waiter quietly served their egg drop soup. He tasted his soup and nodded in appreciation before the waiter left. "Our syndicate agreed to purchase a small…Caribbean island. Little Saint James in the Virgin Islands."

"An island?" Jake's Chinese porcelain spoon paused halfway to his mouth. "What for?"

"It is such a relaxing place to enjoy ourselves."

"I'll bet." Jake slurped up his soup. "Doing what?"

"Oh, you know. The usual."

"I don't want to know, do I?"

"Personally, I enjoy walking on the beach in the morning. It is very relaxing."

"And at night?"

Jhing Xho stared down into his soup and smiled.

"You aren't—no, forget it. The Caribbean is a long, long way outside of my jurisdictional sandbox."

Jhing Xho nodded.

They finished their soup. The waiter cleared their bowls away.

"But the syndicate wants its money back."

"Of course." Jhing Xho crossed the fingers of his hands on the table in front of him. "It is a matter of pride."

"Pride?"

"We have our own sense of honor."

"Of course." Jake leaned back in his chair. "Okay. Forget the syndicate. Who took it?"

"Well, our sources in your department told us The Baron helped himself to our money."

"Your sources?"

"But Maddie shot and killed him. Correct?"

"That she did. He hit the river at terminal velocity."

"And they recovered his body."

Jake nodded. "Eventually."

"So, tell me, then. If it is not Q, who is spending our money?"

The waiter returned and served their family-style meal of Szechuan Chicken, Mongolian Beef, pork fried rice, and egg rolls.

"This meal may be a little bit spicy." Jhing Xho winked.

"Not my first rodeo."

"Jake, if he is not Q…and he is not the Baron…"

"Don't worry. We'll find out who it is."

"If you do not find this person…we will."

"Q is definitely going to be disappointed in that."

"And what about you?"

Jake smiled. "Please pass the Szechuan Chicken."

~~~

King Kandy and the Gingerbread Men

EC walked up behind Kim at her small cubicle desk in Exit Alley. She busied herself stacking and moving papers back and forth on her desktop. "Hey, what are you doing here so late?"

"Catching up."

"With what?"

"Never mind." Kim looked around the Exit Alley offices. "Where's Jake?"

"He had a meeting."

"A meeting?"

"Yeah. Anyway…" EC held up a stack of papers. "Do you think you could take a look at these? They're papers from Monique De La Croix's room. They're in Chinese."

Kim frowned at EC.

"Jake said you know how to speak it."

Kim held out her hand and took the papers. "You got a warrant for these?"

"Exigent circumstances. It might tell us where she is. I think they have something to do with Mitchell's company."

She shook her head, then paged through the papers quickly as EC stood close behind. Kim peered over her shoulder. EC backed away. Kim got up and walked over to the conference table shuffling through the papers, followed by EC.

"What kind of meeting?"

"In AsiaTown." EC gazed up at the ceiling. "Somebody he knows down there."

"About the case?"

"Not sure. Sometimes I don't want to know everything. It's easier that way."

"Jhing Xho?" Kim looked over at EC.

He shrugged. "That'd be my guess."

Kim shook her head. She started reading the papers closely, one at a time. As she finished, she set them down arranged in neat rows on the conference table.

EC found his way to a nearby chair and watched Kim. "What do they say?"

"Were there any other papers?"

"There was another folder with shipping documents." EC held it up.

"So, the *Emma Maersk?*"

"Looks like they have a container coming over from China on that ship. Into Los Angeles. They have another coming into Vancouver." EC flipped through the pages in his folder. "It's on the *Marco Polo.*"

"What's in the containers?"

"Can't be sure. I'm guessing tech stuff of some sort, since that's what they do. But Wally and I can't make heads or tails of the Bills of Lading or the packing lists. I'm hoping there is something about it in there." EC pointed at the papers on the conference table.

"Huh…" Kim returned to the documents, reading and sorting them into even more piles.

"What are those stacks all about?" EC asked.

"Just give me some time."

EC slouched back in his chair. His eyes wandered aimlessly about Exit Alley.

"What do you know about Jhing Xho?" Kim asked.

"He walks on the other side of the street. It's like the Mafia. Everybody knows who the bosses are down there, but they all seem to, you know, move freely about the cabin."

"And Jake?"

"We definitely meet a lot of different kinds of people in our line of work. They seem to get along. It was back when Jake worked Robbery/Homicide before coming to Exit Alley. He had a murder case in AsiaTown and the victim was the son of a friend of a friend of Jhing."

"And Jake solved it?"

"Yeah. He did. The guy's rotting away in Lucasville."

"So, BFFs, then."

"Like I said, you meet a lot of people…"

Kim set down the last of the papers. "Hmmm."

"So, what is that all about?"

"I'm not really sure…it is…very odd."

"How's that?"

"There are printed emails, some memos, what looks like telephone recording transcriptions—with numbers and dates and times—and, I think, transcribed notes—those might be De La Croix's." Kim pointed at the different piles of paper as she spoke. "Does she speak Chinese?"

"Don't know. We didn't do a deep dive on her, but I'm assuming, maybe so. She came back from Hong Kong the day after Mitchell was killed."

"And she's part of A.V. Meridian, right?"

"Minority owner. Along with Mitchell and Mitchell's

uncle—on his father's side."

Kim stood over the conference table tapping her fingers on a stack of papers on the table and nodding her head. "And not the Senator?"

"But that doesn't mean he's not getting a piece of the pie somehow. After all, it is his name they are trading on."

"I hate that sneaky, political, underhanded stuff."

"Don't we all."

"Anyway, these documents are very cryptic. The emails from third parties all have the address headers, with the mail servers, Message-IDs, Sender Policy Frameworks, and DKIMs in them—"

"What are DKIMs?" EC asked.

"Domain Key Identified Mail codes. They allow organizations to check the cryptographic signatures to ensure untampered transit of the message. It ensures the ownership of the message."

EC shook his head.

"Yeah, you guys don't really need Q to sort out all this stuff."

"And?"

"But the replies—which I suspect are from De La Croix or, maybe, Mitchell—are just the content responses. No domains. No mail servers. No nothing."

"So, for her or Mitchell…or A.V. Meridian, they are untraceable?"

"Yup. Which leads me to believe that this file—except for the incriminating email evidence on the other side—can't be electronically traced."

"An insurance policy?" EC asked.

"Yeah, but for what?"

"What do the papers say?"

"Not really sure. It's all in some kind of weird code. I can't figure out what they are talking about."

"How's that?"

Kim picked up the first stack of papers on the conference table. She scanned her finger across the page. "Here, they talk about hippopotamuses. Right here. What does that mean?"

"Hippopotamuses?"

"This Chinese person, Liu Rongfeng, says in her email that delivering to the Zhongtang Warehouse in Dongguan on the expected date should be no problem."

"Where is Dongguanon?"

"It's in the Pearl River Delta, about fifty miles north of Hong Kong. I think it's one of the top five cities in China for exporting products."

"Do they have hippopotamuses there?"

"Not so much. It's China, not Africa."

EC let out a heavy sigh.

"Here—and this is a reply to Liu, I think from De La Croix, but, again, the email header is missing—she asks about the great appetites of the river horses. And whether their hunger could be fully satisfied." Kim flipped back a few pages. "There is no reply, but later a few days after the email, in a telephone transcript, it looks like Rongfeng says that all the marbles have been well placed along the path for the hippopotamuses."

"I don't get it."

"Me, neither." Kim set down the papers in the first stack and picked up the second. "And then in these notes from a week later, De La Croix writes that the Bonbons and Jujubes are safe on the EM and MP."

"The container ships."

"Oh, yeah. The *Emma Maersk* and the *Marco Polo*. She said they're on the way to King Kandy and the Gingerbread Men."

"What in the hell are the Bonbons and the Jujubes?"

"Evidently they are the *Golden Marbles.*" Kim shuffled through another stack of papers. "Here, she says, the golden marbles must move without being swallowed and forever lost."

"Oh, you mean like the kids' game?"

"What are you talking about?"

"Hungry Hungry Hippos." EC shook his head. "So that makes the hippos what? Customs? Or law enforcement maybe? Gee, thanks for that image. Bad enough getting called pigs. What's with the fat animal jokes always?"

"What are you talking about?"

"You've got this plastic board game with hippo heads on it that are trying to swallow up a bunch of marbles in a crazy feeding frenzy. Whoever gets the golden marble wins," EC said.

"Kids' games?"

"I've watched my nieces and nephews play it."

"So, what's the deal with the candy kings…and bonbons? Soft chocolate candies—with liqueur or fruit in the middle? What are those exactly? And who do you think Princess Frostline is? De La Croix?"

"Don't forget the gingerbread men. It sounds like another kids' game: Candy Land."

"None of this sounds high-tech to me."

"It's got to mean something else."

"When does the *Emma Maersk* hit Los Angeles?"

EC looked through the shipping papers. "Probably later

this week."

"Should we alert Customs?"

"Yeah…but that's not going to help us find De La Croix."

~~~

The Tunnel

When Jake signed into the crime scene and slid under the sprawled out yellow tape at the entrance to the tunnel, Kim and Wally stood under the halogen lights, staring at the shadowy, crumpled heap of the victim. EC bent taking a photo of the barcode on Robbie Bennington's back.

Kim looked up at Jake. "So, where've you been?"

"I was in AsiaTown with our good friend Jhing Xho."

"Sharing old times?"

"Something like that. He sends his regards by the way."

"Oh, great."

Jake pointed at the corpse. "Who's this guy?"

"We interviewed him. He's another one of Fat Tony's clients. Got a townhouse in Battery Park." Wally pointed to the apartments and townhouses south over his shoulder. "Looks like he was heading down to the Beach House party at Edgewater."

EC stood up over the body. "Maybe the perp really hates fat lawyers."

"Or maybe just Fat Tony's special collection of pervs," Wally said.

"There's a whole boatload of pedos out there. Why pick on Fat Tony's pride?" Jake asked. "There's got to be another connection. Have we looked at the victims?"

"Some of that info was sealed," said EC.

"Maybe we need to *unseal* it."

"Gonna talk to Q?" EC asked.

Jake looked at Kim. "You want to do it?"

She frowned at him.

"Yeah, I didn't think so." Jake sent a quick text message to Q. He ended it with, *We need to talk.*

Kim crossed her arms across her chest and scowled at him. "What about Mitchell. No victim with him. And not a client of Mr. Elliot either."

"Yeah. Good point." Jake's phone rang. He looked down and saw Maddie's name on the screen. "Gee, I wonder what the FBI wants." He answered the call, heading back out of the tunnel, sliding under the crime scene tape, and walking up the ramp towards Battery Park. "Miss me yet?"

"Always and forever, you putz."

"What's with all the wind noise? Where are you?"

"I'm walking down Pennsylvania Avenue. I needed a little privacy."

"Okay…"

"Had any visitors lately?" Maddie asked.

"You mean in dark suits, polished Oxford shoes, starched white shirts, and red power ties?"

"Monique De La Croix—you know she's missing."

"EC and Wally are following up on it."

"Well, Senator Scofield's Chief-of-Staff came by our offices today and the Senator seems to have a keen interest in her current whereabouts."

"Personal or professional? Or is he just another concerned citizen?"

"You are funny, Jake. Rumors here have it that the two share more than Mitchell in common. She wasn't at Mitchell's funeral."

"We didn't see her in our surveillance—at the church or the cemetery. Thought it was strange, so that's why the boys started running her down," Jake said. "Her room at the Marriott seems to have been empty a couple of days. Her laptop was locked, but they copied some papers—"

"With a warrant?"

"Do you really want me to answer that?"

"Jake…"

"There were shipping papers for two containers coming into Los Angeles and Vancouver."

"What's in them?"

"No clue. They also snagged some papers written in Chinese. Maybe my new partner can help sort that out." Jake looked over his shoulder and saw Lt. Sands walking his way with two men dressed in dark suits, polished Oxford shoes, starched white shirts, and red power ties beside him. "Uh-oh…"

"What's that?"

"Lt. Sands. He's got two Feebs in tow—*great.*"

"After twenty-four hours, kidnapping is assumed to be a federal offense."

"Yeah, yeah, yeah—the Lindberg Act." Jake held up his index finger at Lt. Sands, then pointed at his phone. "Looks like my undivided attention is being requested by my boss. Hey, what do you know about buying an island in the Virgin Islands?"

"Who me? Why would I know anything about that?"

"Check it out, it's called Little Saint James."

"Why?"

"Just do it—*please?* Oh, look. Lt. Sands just put his hands on his hips. You know what that means. Gotta go." Jake hung up.

"Hey, Lieu. What's up."

Lt. Sands glanced at the agent on his left, then right. "Got a minute?"

"For you, *anything.*"

"Special Agent Knox," said the Feeb on Lt. Sands' right.

"Special Agent Wilcox," said the Feeb on the left.

Jake shook hands with both. "Monique? Right?"

Lt. Sands smiled knowingly at Jake.

The agents looked at one another.

"The Senator, huh." Jake shook his head sympathetically.

"We understand Ms. De La Croix has been missing for fifty-four hours," Knox said.

"Well, she wasn't at St. John's for the funeral and was a total no-show at Mitchell's gravesite, but I don't know if she's actually been kidnapped. Who told you that?" Jake asked.

"I think the agents are officially here to help us," said Lt. Sands.

"Sure, sure, sure…but, look, I have a murder victim to tend to over there. Besides, I really think you need to talk to Wally. He's got the lead on De La Croix. He's here, too. So, let me get him for you." Jake headed down towards the murder scene. He waved back at Lt. Sands and the two FBI agents before he disappeared into the tunnel.

"So, was that Maddie?" EC asked. "How's she doing?"

"What have you guys got on De La Croix?" Jake asked as he walked up. "Quickly, please."

"I showed Kim the papers from the Marriott and she said most of it seems to be some kind of code played out with kids' games—so, they must be trying to smuggle something in on the container ships," EC said.

"Kids games?" Jake asked.

"Yeah, like, what, Hungry Hippos and Candy Land," Kim said. "Messed up stuff about paying off customs agents to get the stuff in or out—whatever it is. We still couldn't figure out what is actually in them."

"But it's going to King Candy and the gingerbread men—whoever that is," EC said.

Jake looked at EC, then at Kim. He looked at Wally and asked, "What do you know about this?"

Wally rolled his head back and threw up his hands helplessly. "I got nothing."

"Okay. Perfect. Come on."

"What?"

"Come on," Jake motioned Wally to walk back up the tunnel with him. "You are going to talk to the FBI agents with Lt. Sands."

"What? No—NO! NO!" Wally stopped in his tracks. "Come on, man."

"You don't know anything, right?"

"Not really."

"*Perfect*. We don't need those guys in our way. Just tell them some story about, you know, the kid games stuff. That should keep them confused—but don't say anything about all the papers you pulled out of the hotel room, okay? If I take EC up there, he'd spill it all."

"Papers? What papers?"

"Exactly."

"You think this is a good idea?" Wally asked.

"Best one I have for now."

"Is Sands going to get hacked off at me?"

"He's got no love for them." They walked up out of the

tunnel. Jake waved at the agents. He pointed at Knox and said, "This is Wilcox, and that over there is Knox."

Wilcox frowned.

"No, no. I'm Knox."

"Well, this is Detective Wally. He'll be able to help you guys out with Monique. Right now, I've got a dead body that's not going to wait forever."

"Jake," Lt. Sands said.

"Honest, Monique is his case."

Wally scowled at Jake.

He winked back and headed down the ramp to the tunnel again. Behind him, he heard the ever so faint southern drawl of Kristie from 5 Alive News.

"Oh, Lt. Sands…"

Jake looked back and saw the harsh LED lights on a video camera over his shoulder.

"It appears this is now the fifth victim of the Barcode Baron Strangler is that correct?"

Jake groaned, then slipped under the crime scene tape and back into the tunnel.

~~~

The Triad

Jake watched the glowing neon sunset over the water from a bench at the top of the bluff at Lakewood Park.

Q walked up from behind and sat down at the far end of the bench.

The western horizon's edge slowly swallowed the bright orange star.

Jake sighed.

"What?" Q asked. "No green flash?"

"I keep looking. *Every…single…time,* but, no. No such luck."

"I think it's an urban myth."

"Ye of little faith."

"Yup. That'd be me." Q smirked. "But you knew that, right?"

Jake looked over at Q. "Did you leave your iNode and your phone in the Tesla?"

"One of *those* kinds of meetings?"

Jake turned back where the sun had disappeared and squinted. "That would be correct."

"I always like a little intrigue."

"Do you?"

"So, do you want to know about the victims of our victims?"

"We'll get to that. What do you know about the Triad?"

"As in the Chinese mafia?" Q looked at Jake. He narrowed his eyes. "Ah, why?"

"They call them the 'Heaven and Earth Society.' Seem to have a quaint fondness for meat cleavers."

"And that should worry me?"

"It might. The four hundred and fifty million dollars we've been chasing happens to have once belonged to a certain…*Syndicate* of prominent AsiaTown individuals."

"Well, this information certainly saddens me."

"And did I tell you that Internal Affairs is sniffing around about it, too?"

"How do you know that?" Q asked.

"Kim's brother is in IA and he's been bugging her about it."

"You trust her?"

Jake looked at Q, then back at the darkening horizon. "I do. And I hear he's a real…*asshat.*"

"Oh, yeah? Who says that?"

"Kim."

"*Super.*" Q slouched down on the bench. "This just keeps getting better and better all the time."

"I thought you liked a little intrigue."

"A little. Not a tsunami."

"You're not giving up, are you?" Jake asked.

"You mean between the Chinese mafia and Internal Affairs? I sure am thinking about it."

"Nah—don't go all weak-kneed on me. Besides, you aren't on the police payroll anymore."

"But you are."

"Come on. It'll be fun."

Q stood up. "Are you nuts?"

"Yeah, maybe." Jake stood up, too. "Let's walk."

"Doesn't this place close at dark?"

Motherless Children

"What are you worried about? I'm a cop."

They walked along the path at the top of the face of the bluff towards the S-turning ramp leading down the cliff to the break wall.

"So, who do you hate more? The Triad or Internal Affairs?" Q asked.

"That's easy. The Triad. IA doesn't carry meat cleavers. I like being connected at the wrists and ankles."

"And what are we going to do, then?"

"I don't really have any friends in Internal Affairs, you know? So first, you need to get a rundown on Kim's brother. See what he's really up to and who he hangs out with. I'm not so worried about him, but we need to know. Okay? Shouldn't take you more than fifteen or twenty minutes. Then, we have to do a little homework on the Syndicate."

"How do we do that?"

"Start by looking into Jhing Xho."

"Okay, how do you spell it?"

"J-H-I-N-G…X-H-O. Got it?"

Q closed his eyes and let it sink into his memory banks. "Yeah, yeah. I got it."

"You sure?"

Q pointed at his temple. "Photographic memory."

"Well, what do you know."

"And who is Jhing Xho?"

"He's a local Dragonhead—head of his clan."

"And you know him how?"

"Oh, we're the bestest buddies. I had dinner with him the other night and he told me about the syndicate. They were planning on using the money to buy an island in the Caribbean. A little getaway for themselves, I guess."

"And he knows about *me* digging around the crypto exchanges looking for his money?" Q asked.

"He knows you're looking. So is he. And I'll bet all the other Dragonhead-types out there have their little genius M.I.T. minions humping the Internet trying to get their hands on it, too."

Jake and Q turned down the tree-lined switchback ramp down to the shoreline walkway. At the bottom, Jake turned right and they went to the end of the promenade. The Cleveland skyline began to glow in the twilight.

"You know I'll get it first," Q said.

"Yeah. I do." Jake smiled at Q. "I'm not scared. I have great confidence in you."

"Then what?"

"We should probably know who else is in on the Syndicate. Got to know all the players. But I think Jhing is up to something more. After all, Mitchell was killed in AsiaTown—*his* backyard. Things don't go down like that without permission, you know? *His* permission. It's his turf. So, the big question is how were Mitchell and Jhing involved?"

"What's the main source of Jhing's income?"

"Loan sharking, prostitution, protection, and smuggling."

"Drugs?" Q asked.

"No, as a matter of fact. Though it's very profitable, he steers clear of it. Too much wetwork involved for his tastes. But maybe smuggling other stuff is what Mitchell was doing. He and his partner, De La Croix, were recently visiting Hong Kong. Maybe he was using Jhing to move things into the country. Can you track the shipments of A.V. Meridian over the past two or three years and find out where they ended up?"

"Should be doable. You think he was sending it into AsiaTown?"

"Maybe…maybe. Check with EC and Wally. They said there are two ships coming into port in the next week or so. It would be interesting to track that inventory to see if it shows up in one of Jhing's warehouses."

"What's on the ships?"

"Don't know."

"Okay, but what about the money?" Q asked.

"I've got Maddie checking into that whole buying an island thing."

They turned and wandered west along the promenade behind the break wall, winding up around the Solstice Steps to the top of the bluff again. The last of the twilight was fading. They moved through growing pools of yellowed LED lights from the street lamps.

"So we have the Triad, Internal Affairs, the good guys—that would be you and me—right?" Q asked. "And a player to be named later, who has somehow actually got their hands on the bitcoins."

"And you don't know who is spending it."

"No, I don't. They're running it through tumblers."

"What's that?"

"They break up the bitcoins and swap them out with pieces parts of other ones to break the traceability of the blockchain. Makes it tough to follow the transactions."

"It's like a Rubik's Cube trying to fit these puzzle pieces together, you know?"

"What's a Rubik's Cube?" Q asked.

"Never mind."

"And when we get the money and don't turn it over to the Triad, Jhing Xho and his syndicate friends are going to be very, very upset," Q said.

"We just need to figure out how to run between the raindrops, huh?"

"And how is that?"

"I've got an idea or two. No need to worry. Just find out what going on with Jhing and A.V. Meridian. I think there's something there"

"This is going to work, isn't it?" Q asked.

"Trust me, I know what I'm doing. Now, what about our victims' victims?"

They followed the lakefront west and back up the slope to the top of the bluff. Jake and Q found another park bench and sat down.

"Well, here's an interesting thing. They are all Catholic school girls."

"Do tell."

"Saint Joseph's, Beaumont, and Magnificat."

"Magnificat? That's where Maddie went to high school."

"That one was Paul Whistler's victim. A Junior there. Played on the girl's field hockey team, lacrosse, and swimming. She looks pretty good in her school pics. I've got photos on my phone." Q pointed back at the parking lot.

"That's okay for now. I'll look later."

"She tried to pass herself off as twenty-two in the Bistro to get drinks and I guess Whistler took an...*interest*. I've got to admit, she fills out her swimsuit pretty well, but you know Whistler. He knew, for sure, she was underaged and was probably pulling a Travis Bickle thing on her."

Motherless Children

"And the others?"

"Bennington hit on a Beaumont Senior at Edgewater park and took her back to his place in Battery Park. Burr tried to pick up a freshman from Saint Joseph's Academy at Kamm's Corner. I don't think Fat Tony would have gotten him off before he got killed and barcoded."

"But the Catholic schoolgirl thing, huh?" Jake pondered as he stared out at the lake. "That's weird."

A coyote wandered out in front of them. It stopped and eyed Jake and Q, before loping over to the wire fence and scurrying down the bluff.

The Triple Horn

The bell on the Moonglow Shoppe rang as the front door opened.

"I'll be right there. Just feel free to look around," Amanda called out from her office in the back.

When she came out a short, slender man with dark black hair, dressed in an oddly shiny suit, was browsing around the front of the shop.

"Is there something in particular…" Amanda noticed two much larger men standing outside on either side of the front door. "…you are looking for?"

"Yes, please." The Chinese man turned around. "How are you today, Amanda?"

"I am…okay…mister, ah…"

"Jhing Xho." He smiled and walked up to the counter. "You have a very nice shop here. Many very nice items for sale."

"Do I know you?" Amanda asked.

"Oh, no. I would not think so. I have never been here before."

"But…"

"I own some shops in AsiaTown. Of course, we have our own culture."

"Of course, but—"

"Our own ways." Jhing Xho stood up straight with his hands clasped behind his back. He looked her in the face and smiled.

Amanda slowly smiled back.

"I would like to see that item, there." He pointed down at the driftwood necklace display. "Please."

Amanda looked down and saw him pointing at the same necklace with the Triple Horn of Odin pendant she had given Wally. She looked back up and smiled. "Yes. Of course."

She took the necklace off the display and held it out towards Jhing Xho with the pendant in her palm.

Jhing Xho leaned over and looked at the Triple Horn. He nodded. He stood back up. "May I, please?"

"Yes. Of course."

He gently picked up the necklace and held it in front of his eyes. "I find these symbols fascinating. Do you?"

Amanda nodded.

"I have a friend who was very enamored with this icon here. What does it mean to you?"

"It is—it is from the Vikings originally. It is called the Triple Horn of Odin." Amanda cleared her throat. "He was one of their gods and by drinking out of one of the horns—drinking the mead, the mead of poetry—it gave knowledge and wisdom."

"Yes. Knowledge. Wisdom." Jhing Xho set the necklace down on the countertop. "And it is important about the number three, too? Is it not?"

Amanda glanced at the men outside the front door.

Jhing Xho looked over his shoulder at his bodyguards. "Oh, yes. Pay them no mind. They are my…drivers."

"Sure."

"And you are good with numbers, too. So I hear."

"What?"

"Numbers are very important to the Chinese people, too. You know, numerology."

Motherless Children

Amanda nodded slowly.

"Yes, so many things in common." Jhing Xho grinned.

Amanda smiled back nervously.

"May I buy this item, please?"

"Yes. Yes, of course."

Amanda rang up the sale, put the necklace in a box, bagged it, and handed it to Jhing Xho.

"Thank you so much."

"You are very welcome."

Jhing Xho turned and began to leave. At the door, he stopped and turned back to tell her, "Please tell my friend, Jake, I said hello."

Then he left with his bodyguards.

~~~

Magnificat Blue Streaks

"I don't get it," Kim said, sitting with her elbows on her knees and her chin in her palms, staring at the playing field.

"It's lacrosse," Jake said. He leaned back against the chain-link fence at the top of the Rini Family Bleachers.

"I know that, you moron. But why are we here?"

Jake pointed at the Magnificat attackmen in blue jerseys charging their opponent's goal. "There. Number seventeen."

"Yeah…*and?*"

"A person of interest."

"How so?"

Jake looked at Kim and smirked. "Do you really want to know?"

"Q?"

"Kind of."

Kim looked back at the field and huffed.

"I don't think the Avon Eagles have a chance."

"It's a hockey game in slow-motion." Kim watched number seventeen, reading her name off the jersey. "And what is it about Ms. Walsh that makes her so *interesting?*"

"The late Paul Whistler. He of nubile inclinations."

The Blue Streaks scored a goal. The team gathered and cheered.

"See? I told you so," said Jake. "You know, you are going to have to talk to her after the game."

"Why me?" Kim asked.

"Come on…I don't need that kind of awkward conversation added on to my permanent record."

"Great."

"The game's almost over. You should get down there so we can move along with our day."

"You don't want to listen in?"

"I trust you."

Kim got up and carefully stepped down the bleacher seats to the playing field.

Jake leaned back against the screen with his hands behind his head and watched.

Kim called the coach over and whispered in her ear. She discreetly showed her the police badge hung on her belt.

"Alicia!" the coach called out and waved her over. "I'll leave you to it."

"I am a detective," Kim whispered when the coach walked away.

"What do you want?"

"Let's get a little privacy, okay?" Kim took a step to the north, away from the other players walking off the field.

Alicia looked around. "But shouldn't my parents be here?"

"Okay. We can certainly set up a meeting and have them come down with you to the police station, if you want, and we can talk all about Paul Whistler. And, you know, get it all on tape." Kim smiled. "But, really, I just have a few quick questions. That's all."

"Well, okay. I guess." Alicia stepped up to Kim and they began walking north. She dragged her lacrosse stick behind her.

Kim smiled at the other Blue Streak players as they passed by.

"How did you get my name?"

"I am investigating the death of Mr. Whistler," Kim said. "And your name came up."

Alicia scratched the back of her neck and pulled nervously at her jersey. "I didn't have anything to do with it—him getting killed. I don't know anything about it."

"Of course. I know that."

They took a few more steps.

"I was almost old enough, you know? It's just that my dad…"

"What about him?"

"He didn't do anything either. Well, I mean, he went to a lawyer downtown?"

"Who was that? Mr. Elliot?"

"No. A prosecutor guy he knows. My dad works for the city."

"And the prosecutor…"

"He called the police and they eventually arrested Paul. Well, I mean they had to talk to me first. With my dad there. I didn't want to, you know. And then they arrested him."

"They were going to press charges?" Kim asked.

Alicia nodded. "They didn't need to do it. It was only going to be another few months. But no. That's not what my dad wanted. Oh, no, not Mister Catholic Man and all."

"And then?"

"I couldn't see him. I couldn't talk to him. And, I don't know what happened. Then he was dead. And I don't know what happened."

"I'm sorry." Kim looked down at Alicia. She was borderline Iris and Lolita: alluringly young and innocent—but then again, not so much. "What does your father do for the city?"

"He works for the Streets Department. He's a supervisor or something."

"What does he do?"

"I don't know. Supervises." Alicia shrugged.

"Did you know of anyone who wanted to kill Mr. Whistler?"

Alicia shook her head. "No. I didn't know his friends or his enemies or anyone else in his life. He had an apartment over the Bistro. We'd meet there. Of course, my dad wanted him thrown in jail. For a long, long time. But he'd never kill anyone."

Kim stopped. She turned Alicia around and began heading back towards the bleachers and the school buildings. "Did you ever meet Mr. Whistler's lawyer?"

She shook her head.

"Did, ah…" Kim looked at the empty playing field.

"Paul was really nice. We just went down there for some fun one Friday night."

"We? Who's that?"

Alicia kicked at the turf. "I don't want to say."

"Yeah. Okay."

"But he was really, really nice to me. I think he knew."

"That you were fifteen?"

"He didn't care. He just didn't care."

"I'll bet he didn't."

✳✳✳~ ~ ~✳✳✳

As Kim and Alicia talked, Jake watched the Magnificat players meet up with their parents and leave. The Eagles boarded a school bus to go back to Avon.

On the far side of the field, in the parking lot by the tennis courts, a man stood watching the players. He stayed after the field had emptied and watched Kim and Alicia walk down the sideline and back.

Jake noticed and sat forward. Then, he stood.

The man looked at Jake, then climbed on a black Kawasaki Ninja ZX motorcycle. The engine revved up into a high-pitched whine as he quickly spun around to exit out the front entrance, disappearing into traffic on Hilliard Boulevard.

He was too far away for Jake to read the license plate number.

I Ain't Superstitious

Wally leaned against the back wall of Exit Alley, waiting. He hummed the melody of a Howlin' Wolf song, "I Ain't Superstitious."

He stopped humming and stood up straight when he saw the black Mustang pull into the police parking lot. He watched Jake and Kim get out and head his way.

"Got a minute?" he asked when Kim and Jake stepped up.

"I know. I know. I owe you big time for giving you up to the Feds," Jake said.

"No—I mean, yeah, but…" Wally looked over at Kim. He cocked his head to the side and let out a big sigh.

"Oh, I get it. *Girl talk,* huh?" Kim snickered and said to Jake, "I'll meet you inside."

Wally and Jake watched Kim use her badge to log into the ACU building locks and go inside.

"What's up?" Jake asked.

Wally took a step closer, standing right next to Jake. He looked down and growled.

Jake squinted up into his face. "You're mad. Okay, what is it? Out with it."

"Moonglow," Wally sneered. "Why is Amanda getting visitors from AsiaTown?"

"And who's that?"

"Your friend, Jhing Xho." Wally pressed his index finger into Jake's chest. "And his two muscle men."

Jake stared down at Wally's hand pushing against his chest. "Do you *mind?*"

"Yeah…right…" Wally put his arm down.

"What was he doing there?"

"Evidently, he stopped by to tell you, 'Hello.' He talked a bit about numerology…and then he bought one of these." Wally pulled the Triple Horn necklace Amanda had given him out of his pocket and held it up.

"That's the logo for A.V. Meridian."

"Sure is. What's that mean?"

"This one, right?" Jake pointed at the pendant. "Specifically."

Wally nodded. "Yup. This very one. He asked for it."

"Yeah…that's what I was afraid of."

"You know who her dad is, right?"

"Assistant Safety Director or something."

"Or something. That Jhing guy's got some balls on him."

"I'll talk to my sergeant buddy at the Lakewood PD. They'll keep an eye on her."

"What does he want with Amanda?"

"The real question is, how did Jhing find out? Nobody knows she was helping us, right? That she was working with you on the barcodes. You didn't say anything, did you?"

"Nope. Just to you and EC and Kim. Nobody else."

"What about her dad?"

"Sean? Yeah, maybe." Wally squinted his eye and asked, "What about you?"

"Not me."

Wally put his hands on his hips. "And Kim?"

"She's my partner."

"Yeah…and? I know some District Four guys who might be wondering, too."

"Don't go there."

Lt. Sands walked up from the parking lot. He slowed down as he noticed Jake and Wally's confrontation. He stepped over, put his hand on Jake's shoulder, and asked, "Boys…what's going on?"

"Nothing. Nothing at all," Wally said, turning and stepping back from Jake. He looked over at Jake and shook his head. "I don't like this. I don't like it one bit."

"Like what?" Lt. Sands asked.

"Complications," Jake said.

"You mean besides the five dead bodies we got piled up? Just what I need," Lt. Sands said. "Now what?"

"The Triad," Jake said. "Jhing Xho."

"You don't want to get Organized Crime involved do you?"

"Oh, great," Wally moaned. "More party-goers."

"No. We don't need their help. It's just murder," Jake said.

"Don't forget kidnapping," said Lt. Sands. He re-knotted his tie. "Ms. De La Croix and our Federal Friends from Lakeside Avenue helping us out on that one."

"Oh, yeah." Wally rubbed his forehead.

"So, how does Jhing Xho fit in?" Lt. Sands asked.

"Show him," said Jake.

Wally held up the Triple Horn pendant. "This."

"Which is…"

"That is the logo for the Senator's son's import/export business. A.V. Meridian," Jake said. "I think there's a connection there, between Jhing and Mitchell."

"How's that?"Lt. Sands asked.

"Not exactly sure."

Lt. Sands shook his head.

"You going to tell him?" Wally asked.

"Tell me what?"

"You know Sean in the Security Director's office at Public Square? His daughter was helping us out and Mr. Triad found out about it."

"Helping out?"

"She solved the barcodes for us," Wally said.

"How's that?"

"Well, ah…"

"That doesn't matter, really," Jake said. "Somebody, somewhere around here is leaking like a sieve."

"Who?"

"Yeah…*who?*"

~~~

You Deserve a Break Today

"Here. Eat a cheeseburger." He tossed the McDonald's bag over to the bed where Monique De La Croix lay curled up in a fetal position facing the wall. "Nobody likes a skinny Santa."

She sat up slowly. "Ugh! I need real food."

He leaned against the refrigerator doorway and slurped up the last of his chocolate milkshake from the bottom of his cup through a straw. "Real food? Who do you think you are, anyway?"

"You don't know who I am, do you?"

"I know enough. I know about the old man."

"The old man?"

"The Senator." He grinned. "And his son."

"Are you the one? The one who killed him."

"Not in so many words. But I did…set things in motion. Like the others."

Monique leaned back against the headboard. "Why?"

"Why?"

She nodded.

"Hmm. I don't know. Let me ask, where did you go to school? Some private girls' academy or something, I'll bet. Maybe even a parochial school. And then some exclusive, private college, right?"

"Yeah. Maybe—so what?"

"Did you meet many men there…like the Senator?"

Monique silently winced.

"Teachers? Professors?" He nodded. He smiled. "Yeah. I thought so."

She opened the McDonald's bag and pulled out a quarter pounder with cheese. She opened the box and took a small bite.

"Not so bad, now, is it?"

Monique shrugged. "But, why?"

"I know about guys like the Senator. I know how they are. And who they are. You do, too. Right?"

Monique broke off a small bit of the burger with her hand, put it in her mouth, and slowly chewed.

"Yeah, I thought so."

She swallowed. "Are you going to kill him, too?"

"I don't know. Kind of hard to kill a Senator. I might have something else in mind."

"Like what?"

"I believe his wife is still here, in town."

"Are you going to kill her?"

He shrugged his shoulders. "Would you like that?"

Monique scowled at him.

He put his fingers to his lips and whistled.

A man appeared behind him and stared at Monique.

She recoiled, though his face, expressionless, was vaguely familiar. Like an old-time actor—maybe Tom Hanks. But the eyes were dead, like a snake's black eyes.

The synthoid was dressed only in Under Armour gym shorts. She noticed the front panel in his chest was missing, exposing the wiring harnesses, control modules, hydraulic lines, and muscle actuators.

"You might want to keep Ms. De La Croix company for a little while," he said, moving aside to let it into the meat locker.

Motherless Children

It smiled. And stared.

Monique curled up and pushed herself back into the far corner with her feet.

~~~

Hot Type

Jake stood outside his apartment on the back fire escape. He leaned on the railing watching Lake Erie a half-mile away through the trees, drinking from his first mug of coffee for the morning.

"All by your lonesome out here?" Kristie asked as she opened the door and came out onto the fire escape. She pulled the belt tight on her short, silk robe, then sat down on a lawn chair and crossed her legs. She carefully spread out the lapels around her cleavage.

Jake looked over his shoulder at her. He sighed.

"Come on. You can talk to me."

"On the record or off?"

"Depends upon what you tell me, of course." Kristie winked at Jake.

"*Why...why...why...*" He closed his eyes and rubbed them with his fingers.

"Come on. You know exactly why, darlin'." Kristie smiled and pulled the bottom of her robe up higher on her thighs. "So, what's on your mind."

Jake turned around and leaned his back against the rail. "Lt. Sands says you seem to know a lot about our cases—you know like the Battery Park homicide."

"Maybe I do."

"And how is that?"

"Maybe it's just hard work, you know? Nose to the grindstone and all—"

Jake shook his head.

"What? You don't believe me?"

"Not so much."

"And, well, maybe I have some friends. Some in high places. And that takes work, too, you know."

"Like in the Safety Director's Office?"

Kristie tapped her chin with her index finger. "Perhaps so."

"Like who?"

"Wait a minute." She pouted. "Why are you asking all the questions?"

"Because I'm the police?"

"Oh, no. That's not how this works. Fifty-fifty. Even Steven. Like always."

"I don't know."

"Or we could go back to the bedroom." She smiled coyly.

"We could…" Jake took a sip of coffee. "Or maybe Truth or Dare?"

"Honey, I don't have much left to dare with you." She held her arms out in mock surrender.

"Okay. Even Steven."

"Good. You go first."

Jake squinted down at Kristie. "Let's start off easy. What do you know about Kim's brother?"

"Detective Sergeant Rick? In Internal Affairs? Let's see…he seems to be kind of a weasel. Has been stuck there for three-and-a-half years, and when Kim got sideways with those crooks in Narcotics last year, his stock crashed hard. Thought he'd be moving on up the chain of command, but not so much now. He's been trying to recruit Kim into IA to redeem himself, but, hey look, now she's *your* partner. So, how's that working out for the Detective Sergeant? Not so good."

"And what does he know about the four hundred and fifty million dollars that went missing from the law firm during the Baron case?"

"Now, wait a minute. Even Steven, right?"

"Shoot."

"What does Mitchell Scofield have to do with your other victims? The other ones were all sex crime guys, right?"

"Yeah—except for Fat Tony."

Kristie shuddered at the mention of the lawyer's name.

"Me, too. Whistler, Burr, and Bennington all had things for young Catholic school girls. Nothing like that for Scofield that we've found." Jake looked hard at Kristie. "Off the record, right?"

"Yeah…for now. But you are going to have to let me run with this sometime."

"Fair enough—but I'll let you know when, okay?"

She nodded.

"His company, A.V. Meridian, has two shipments coming into Los Angeles and Vancouver from China. Seems to be some serious greasing along the way of Customs officials to get them through when they hit port."

"And what's in the shipping crates?"

"That's the sixty-four-thousand-dollar question."

"But your perps are all local, small-time pervs, right?"

"Right, so where's the connection with China?"

"Maybe AsiaTown?"

"And what do you know about that?" Jake asked.

"About what?"

"Jhing Xho."

"Now there is an interesting fellow." Kristie leaned forward. "He's in the mob—their mob, right?"

"The Triad. So tell me, who's been leaking information on our cases to him from the Department?"

"Oh…so it's your turn again? Well, my guess would be your partner's brother. But I don't think he's really the gray matter behind it all. There's someone else. Higher up, that he's sucking up to. Remember he still wants to climb the corporate ladder."

"Like who?"

"My guess is Sean Corrigan."

"Seriously? The Assistant Security Director?"

Kristie nodded. "Let's just say that Detective Sergeant Rick spends an…*unusual* amount of time in Mr. Corrigan's office."

"That's Wally's guy downtown—his partner from a long while back. And…"

"And what?"

"His daughter. She's the one who solved the barcodes for us. Numerology. She's a—well, it doesn't really matter."

"Come on. Out with it."

Jake scratched the back of his neck and shook his head. "She's a Wiccan."

"Interesting. And what do the barcodes mean?"

"Sorry. Got to keep some things off the table for now. Maybe later."

"Well, now I'm tired of this stupid game." Kristie stood up and slowly pulled open the belt on her robe. She took Jake's hand. "Let's go back inside."

~~~

The Street Department

"We're looking for Kyle Walsh," EC said to the prim, middle-aged receptionist in the Cleveland Street Department lobby.

"And who are you?" she asked without looking up from the computer screen.

"We're the cops," Wally said. He put his elbows on her counter and held out his badge in front of her face.

She looked at him and his badge with disdain, then said, "And…"

"We would like to speak with him," EC said. "Please."

"About what?"

"Police business, ma'am." Wally leaned his head over her workspace and looked at her computer screen. "Solitaire?"

She took a dramatically deep breath, then loudly exhaled. Picking up the phone, she dialed an extension and glared back up at Wally. "There are two policemen here to see you." She listened. "I don't know…okay I'll tell them." She hung up. "He'll be out in a minute."

"Thank you," EC said, smiling politely.

"If you don't mind…" she turned her monitor away from Wally.

A few minutes later, a barrel-chested, red-haired man came out of a back office and headed through the cubicle maze into the lobby. "What's this all about, then?"

Walsh towered over EC as he held out his badge.

Wally looked him eye-to-eye. "Just a little chit-chat."

"About what?"

"Alicia," EC said loud enough for the receptionist to hear.

She lifted her head to listen.

Walsh blushed a bit. He turned and headed back into the cubicle maze. "This way."

EC followed.

"Play the seven of spades on the eight of hearts," Wally said to the receptionist as he walked by.

Walsh led the detectives back to his office and quickly shut the door.

Wally stepped over to the bookshelves and looked over the pictures of Alicia posing in her Magnificat lacrosse uniform, with her swim team, and in her Catholic white pique polo and dark blue skirt.

Walsh watched and grimaced. His right eye twitched a bit. "I thought this was all over. Whistler is dead, right?"

"Yeah, well, that's actually our problem," Wally said, turning around. He stared at Walsh.

"I told you before, that S.O.B. deserved it. Alicia's my only child." Walsh ground his right fist into his left hand. "But it wasn't me, that's for sure—'cause he ended up looking too damn good."

"There were two others," EC said. "Two other Catholic school girls. With two other men."

"I don't know anything about any of that." Walsh walked around behind his desk, turned around, and stared back.

"Didn't say that you did," Wally said.

"Yeah, well…"

"If you didn't kill Whistler, know anyone who might have?"

Wally asked.

Walsh shook his head. "No. No clue."

"You're a maintenance supervisor. How many folks do you have out on the road?" EC asked.

"Fourteen. Why? You don't think one of them…"

"Look, it's all just routine. We just need the names to check out," EC said.

Walsh looked out his window. He scratched his cheek for a moment. "Yeah, ah, I don't know…"

"Mr. Walsh, I get it. Whistler was a predator," EC said. "But his death is an active murder investigation."

Walsh looked down at a picture of Alicia and his wife on his desk. He took a deep breath, then exhaled.

"We're trying to find a serial killer." Wally stepped over to lean on Walsh's desk.

Walsh refused to meet his stare. "I don't want to cause any problems for my people."

EC shook his head. "Kyle…"

"Come on, man," Wally said.

Walsh shrugged his shoulders.

"You know something, don't you?" Wally asked.

"No. No, nothing. I don't…"

"Who is it?" EC asked calmly.

"All I know is that Alicia is safe and that dirtbag is dead. That's all I need to know." Walsh glanced at Wally for just a moment, then stepped over to look out the window again.

Wally stood up. He put his hands on his hips and shrugged at his partner.

EC said in his most official-sounding tone, "Mr. Walsh, if you are hiding any information that could help our case—"

Walsh turned and looked at EC. "Do you have a subpoena?"

"A subpoena? Seriously?" Wally asked. "We all work for the city, pal. We'll just go down to Personnel and get the names."

"Maybe you ought to do that then." Walsh glared at Wally.

"Who is it?" EC asked.

"I'm not causing any problems for anybody," Walsh said. "Got it?"

"Yeah," Wally said. "Got it."

Walsh went to his office door and opened it. "You know the way out, right?"

EC stepped out into the hall.

Wally paused to look Walsh directly in the eye.

Walsh's right eye twitched.

"*Right…*" Wally muttered. "I know nothing."

~~~

Ian pulled his city-marked pickup truck into the Bratenahl neighborhood and wound his way back to Lakeshore Boulevard.

His cell phone pinged with a text message from his boss, Kyle Walsh: *Call me.*

Ian ignored it.

He slowed as he drove by Senator Scofield's mansion. The landscapers out front paid him no mind.

After passing by he quickly sped up, then circled around to Eddy Road. He turned south to get on the Shoreway, heading downtown to the butcher shop.

~~~

Brother Rick

Detective Sergeant Rick from Internal Affairs was parallel parked on the side street facing the back of the Glick Building where Jake lived. He held a burner phone to his ear with his eyes closed. He slid down low behind the steering wheel and breathed deeply through the open driver's window. His head was bowed, absorbing the abuse of Assistant Safety Director Sean Corrigan.

"I—I—" Rick stuttered. "But—but…"

"You are Internal Affairs. What did you think was going to happen?" Corrigan demanded.

"But I didn't know—"

"Jesus H. Christ. Grow a brain cell or two, why don't you?"

"I did not know that Amanda was *your daughter.*"

"Did you forget that Jhing Xho is in the mob, for crying out loud? *The mob.* You know how those guys are. And then, of course, he shows up at her shop. What's next? Huh? What? You better get your ass down to AsiaTown and fix this—*right away.*"

Rick was startled by a metallic tap on the rear window. "Huh—What?"

"What?" Corrigan asked.

"Hey, there, Brother Rick." Jake smiled holding his badge out in his left hand and pointing his Colt 1911 forty-five at the back of the detective's head. "Who are you talking to?"

"I'll take care of it, right away—gotta go," Rick said into the phone and hung up.

"Was that Sean?" Jake asked.

"None of your business." Rick sat up straight. He noticed Jake's pistol.

"Oh, I think it might be."

"Are you serious? Drawing your firearm on a fellow officer?" Rick asked. "Did you forget that I'm Internal Affairs?"

"You see, my neighbor, Mrs. Cwiklinski—she lives right over there." Jake pointed at the house across the street. He waved and the front blinds quickly closed. "She's been very concerned about this suspicious individual parked on her street out in front of her house lately."

"And that would be me?" Rick asked.

"Yes. That would be you."

Rick was startled again as the passenger door opened suddenly.

Kim sat down in the front seat. "Just what in the hell are you doing here?"

He looked back at Jake and scowled. "Why did you tell her?"

"It seemed like the right thing to do," Jake said.

"Yeah, well, I don't have to say anything to you."

Kim punched Rick as hard as she could in the arm. "Spill it—*or I will shoot you.*"

"Perhaps you should be aware that we know about…your friendly relationship with Sean Corrigan," Jake said.

"Give me that phone." Kim grabbed the burner phone out of Rick's hand. "Let's just do a quick re-dial."

"NO!" He reached out.

"Easy." Jake pressed his pistol into the back of Rick's head. *"Easy."*

Kim held the phone up, ready to press the call button. "I'll do it."

Rick crossed his arms and stared down into his lap.

"When, exactly, did you turn into such a weasel?" Kim asked.

"You couldn't help me out?" Rick muttered. "I'm family."

"Help you out?" Kim asked. "How?"

"I am going to die in Internal Affairs."

"That's your choice. Not mine," Kim said.

"Get his gun," Jake said. "Then let's go sit down and have a nice friendly, family-like conversation."

Kim reached under Rick's jacket and pulled his Glock out of his shoulder holster.

Jake opened the driver's door and yanked Rick out by his arm. He discreetly pressed his forty-five into Rick's side. "Easy now. Nice and easy."

They walked to the back of Jake's building and went inside. EC sat at the bar. Wally leaned against the pool table facing the front of the building. He turned around to look at Kim, Rick, and Jake as they came in.

"Is this the guy?" Wally asked, scowling down on the detective as he walked by.

"Hey, that's my brother," Kim said.

"You may not know Detective Sergeant *Rick*…from Internal Affairs," Jake said.

Wally followed him around as Jake forced Rick down onto a kitchen chair set out in the middle of the floor.

EC watched from the bar. "He was parked outside?"

"Out back. Mrs. Cwiklinski was kind enough to tell me." Jake looked down at Rick. "You thought I was kidding, didn't you?"

Rick folded his arms across his chest and stared straight ahead, looking at nothing.

Kim walked over and looked down at her brother. "You need to come clean."

"Come clean about what? Are you in on the four hundred fifty million dollars, too?"

Kim looked at Jake. "Okay. Tell me. What's he talking about?"

"The money stolen from Stein, Baylor, and Stein in the Baron case." Rick looked up at Jake. "You know what I mean."

"Is that what Corrigan is after?" Wally asked.

Rick dropped his eyes again.

"Yeah…Maddie and I talked to those guys after it happened," EC said. "Typical cover-your-ass lawyer types."

"Q found the bitcoins. parked in a Cayman Islands account." Jake looked over at Wally. "It belonged to Jhing Xho and some of his friends. They were going to use it to buy an island in the Caribbean."

"And that's why he showed up at the Moonglow shop with his goons?" Wally pointed at Rick. "Did this guy tell Jhing?"

"I did not know Amanda was Sean Corrigan's daughter," Rick huffed.

"What a moron." Wally shook his head. "I ought to—"

"That's my brother," Kim said.

Wally shrugged his shoulders.

"Is that what Q's been looking for on his laptop?" Kim asked Jake.

"Here's the thing…somebody is controlling that money now. There have been some withdrawals—about two hundred and fifty thousand dollars," Jake said.

"But if the Baron is dead…" EC said.

"Yeah. Who is working it now?" Jake answered. "And where is it going?"

"You don't think it's going to our guy, do you?" Kim asked.

"That's the deal with bitcoins. You can't trace them." Jake looked at Rick. "And that's what Corrigan was after, right? The four hundred and fifty million. And that's why he put you onto me, right?"

Rick shook his head.

"I can't believe this," Wally said. "Corrigan? He was my partner."

"Everybody thought it was free money," Jake said. "You just had to find it. And Q did it."

"And Jhing wants it back," EC said.

"I'd say so."

"And Corrigan?" Wally asked.

"The real question is whether the Assistant Safety Director is working with Jhing Xho or on his own." Jake looked at Rick. "What did he promise you? Cause he sure can't just show up in AsiaTown, right? To meet with the mob."

"Maybe I should have my union rep here," Detective Rick said.

Wally laughed out loud.

"Son, I don't think that's how this is going to work," EC said.

Jake started dialing his phone.

"Who are you calling?" Kim asked.

"Lt. Sands," Jake said. "We have Internal Affairs colluding with the Assistant Safety Director to help the Triad. I think that's a bit above my pay grade."

"What about Q?" Kim asked.

"He doesn't need the money. Never did. He's loaded," Jake

said. "He's in it for the sport."

"And you?" Detective Rick asked.

"I've got my Mustang, my man cave, and my job. What more do I need?" Jake's call was answered. "Hey, Lieu, I've got a situation here that needs your personal management oversight…Yeah. Right away."

$$***\sim\sim\sim***$$

Prospecting

Q sat in his Tesla in the parking lot of the Rosewood Grill on Crocker Road watching the Huntington Bank next door. He had traced a part of the last withdrawal of fifty-thousand dollars from the bitcoin account to this location.

At five-thirty, a black Denali pulled up to the front door of the bank. A slender, young blonde girl, maybe seventeen or eighteen, stepped out of the back and went inside.

Q sat up straight and watched closely. Her face was vaguely familiar, though he could not determine why.

He grabbed his Nikon with the 300mm telephoto lens and focused on the doorway. Twenty minutes later, just before closing, she came back out and he quickly fired the camera in burst mode as she got back in the Denali.

As the SUV pulled out into traffic, Q eased onto Crocker Road and followed a few car lengths back. His photographic memory locked in the license plate number.

As the Denali turned east on I90, Q followed and matched their speed, keeping further back in the far-right lane, but close enough to see the tall SUV.

Passing through Rocky River, the Denali sped up and Q weaved into the passing lanes.

Through Lakewood and into Cleveland, the SUV's speed reached 85 miles per hour, until it had to be obvious to the driver that Q's Fusion Red Tesla was following it.

The Denali cut right across four lanes of honking traffic and exited at West Boulevard before Q could react and follow.

Q watched from the overpass as the Denali disappeared south.

Turning east on Lorain Avenue, the SUV slowed to the speed limit. At Randall Road, it turned north, then left right away on Cyrano Court. Stopping behind the abandoned butcher shop, Bill, the Baron's caretaker, got out from behind the wheel and slipped a stack of cash into the rear mail slot.

He got back in and quickly drove away.

~~~

Stakeout

Kim and Jake sat on a park bench in Public Square across from the Safety Department offices. They munched on apples and a bag of warmed cashews.

"Do you think he'll do it?" Jake asked.

"Yeah. He will," Kim answered. "He doesn't really have any other options."

"What will he do after?"

"I don't know."

"He could be a mall cop."

"Hey, be nice," Kim said. "He's still my brother."

Jake nodded and leaned back against the bench.

"So, why are we here?"

"You ever met Sean Corrigan?" Jake held up a picture of the Assistant Security Director printed off the Department's website.

Kim shook her head.

"Yeah, me neither. I just like to know who I'm dealing with."

Jake's phone rang. He looked and saw it was Maddie calling.

"I've got to take this." He handed Kim the picture of Corrigan, stood, and stepped away. "Hey, what's up?"

"Where are you at?" Maddie asked.

"Public Square. With Kim."

"Our bench?"

"No. We're staking out the Safety Director's offices." He

looked at the half-eaten apple in his left hand. "Got a bad apple there."

"Is he involved with your case?"

"Seems so. Where are you? At the office?"

"I walked down to the Mall." Maddie sighed. "I miss being out and about, you know? Doing real police work."

"That's what you get for becoming a federal bureaucrat."

"Don't rub it in. Anyway, I had Customs clear the shipment from A.V. Meridian that came into Los Angeles. It's heading to a warehouse on East 40th Street."

"AsiaTown."

"Yeah. Like you said."

"And they let it through with no problems?"

"Yup. Should be there by the end of the week. I'll text you the tracking number."

"Who owns the warehouse?"

"Looks like a shell corporation. An LLC called Lotus Eaters. The registered agent is Anthony Elliot."

"Fat Tony?"

"Who's that?" Maddie asked.

"One of our victims. He was also the defense attorney for three of our other victims on sex crime charges. Kind of his specialty."

"But you don't know who your perp is, do you."

"EC and Wally think he works in the city Streets Department. They're down at Personnel getting the records."

"Good luck. And you know that island in the Caribbean—Little St. James—the one Jhing Xho is trying to buy? The locals used to call it the Island of Sin. Some billionaire owned it and ran it as a…brothel, I guess—mainly with underaged women. They arrested him on sex trafficking charges in 2019 and the DOJ eventually seized the island. I guess he killed himself in jail and the island eventually passed through a few different owners until it was put back on the market earlier this year."

"Sex trafficking?"

"He had a lot of…*friendly*…*powerful* faces visiting him on the island."

"Like…"

"You know. Rich people. Presidents. Even royalty—if you believe that."

"And the Senator?"

"On the list."

"And he killed himself? In custody?"

"So they say."

"Hmmm…Has Scofield sent his aides down to the FBI lately?" Jake asked.

"I haven't seen them."

"Well, what about De La Croix?"

"Radio silence. The field agents there are working with Lt. Sands, but I haven't heard anything back. Are they getting in your way? I keep waiting for them to ask me about your serial cases."

"No. Sands has held them at bay on that. Thank God. So, the Senator's lost interest?"

"Maybe. Maybe not. I may not be in on the email loops. Yeah, probably not."

Jake noticed Kim stand up and wave at him. She pointed towards the Security Department building. He noticed Sean Corrigan leaving.

"Look, I gotta get going here. How's Wyatt doing?"

Maddie sighed. "Good. You should be around more."

"I know. I know. Maybe when this case breaks, I'll come down."

"Yeah. Okay."

An awkward silence on the line.

"I really have to go," Jake said.

"Okay. Bye."

Jake tossed his apple core in the trash and went back over to Kim. They started following Corrigan as he headed north on Second Street, then turned west on St. Clair Avenue. "Let's split up."

Jake crossed to the opposite side of the street. Corrigan walked three blocks, then turned back toward the lake again on West Sixth Street. Jake caught the crosswalk at St. Clair and followed directly behind him. Kim waited to cross Sixth Street and walked up the opposite sidewalk.

Jake stepped into the doorway of a smoke shop as Corrigan stopped in front of the Barley House Tavern and talked to someone waiting out front. Then they went inside.

Twenty minutes later, Wally stormed back out and headed back towards the station house.

"Wally?" Kim asked when she crossed the street and joined Jake. "For real?"

Jake just watched as Wally cut into a parking lot and disappeared.

~~~

White Chapel

When Kim and Jake got back to Exit Alley, Wally paged through folders from the Personnel Department with EC at the conference table.

Kim looked at Jake, then turned to ask EC, "Any luck?"

"Nothing yet," EC said. He noticed Jake staring intently at Wally. "What's up?"

"Nothing," Jake said, sitting at his desk and shuffling papers aimlessly about.

EC watched for a long moment, then went back to his stack of manila file folders.

Jake's phone pinged with a text message from Q. It was a photo of the blonde girl from Huntington Bank with the message, *Know her?*

Jake studied the picture. She seemed somehow familiar but different. He typed, *Not sure…*

Meet me outside.

"I've got to get some air," Jake said, standing up.

"But you were just outside," EC said.

Jake ignored him and went out the main entrance. He looked up the alleyway heading to the station house. Q was halfway up leaning against the brick wall.

"So, who is she?" Jake asked. He held up his phone with the photo.

"She's got our money," Q said. "She grabbed a chunk of it out of a bank…*in cash.*"

"How much?"

"Fifty thousand."

Jake whistled and looked at the photo on his phone again. "She's familiar somehow."

"Came and left in a big, black Denali."

"Yeah…and?"

"I tried to follow them, but they lost me heading east on I90. The car is owned by White Chapel, LLC." Q showed Jake a pdf of the car's registration certificate.

"The Baron's company?"

Q nodded. "Yeah. Him again."

"How can that be?" Jake looked at the photo on his phone again, scrolling the image of her face out with his fingers to fill the screen. "I wonder…"

"What?"

Her hair was fashionably cut. Her makeup was applied modestly, enhancing her beauty. He finally saw it in her eyes. *"Amy."*

"Not the waitress. The one you…I thought she died."

"Yeah, she did. She got thrown off the Main Avenue Bridge." Jake sighed.

"So, who is this?"

"Amy, the orphan girl Maddie looked after and helped out. She was a witness at one of our murder scenes. The Baron took her as a hostage, too. I thought after that all went down, Maddie got her placed with a family in Westlake."

"That's where the bank was."

"She's older now—eighteen or nineteen? But I see it in her eyes. There was a hard, cutting edge there. Almost reptilian—or no, sharper: hawkish. Always watching. Like she knew way too much for such a young girl."

"What is she doing in the Baron's car?" Q asked. "And what is she doing with his money?"

"Yeah...*what?*"

~~~

Bratenahl

Ian parked his city Streets Department pickup truck down the road from the Senator's lakeside mansion. The setting sun smeared the western sky with pinks, purples, and oranges. From his surveillance, Ian knew the housekeeper was long gone and the only person at home was the Senator's wife. He waited for the downstairs lights to go out.

Wordlessly, via software on his phone, he instructed the synthoid to get out of the truck and proceed, then watched the feed of its CMOS optical sensors through a secure Sawtooth link to his phone.

Monique De La Croix sat beside him helpless, handcuffed and gagged. She watched it disappear into the early twilight, then looked at Ian.

The synthoid cut behind a neighbor's house and effortlessly scaled the six-foot wrought iron fence into the Senator's backyard. It froze behind lilac bushes. The noise gate on the audio input automatically lowered to -48 dB.

Ian could hear crickets in the background.

The synthoid methodically heat-scanned the yard for the Senator's German Shepherd, Major.

Mrs. Scofield despised the Secret Service, the Capitol Police, and private protection guards, often hired by the Senator's staff. Though drive-by security sweeps were scheduled past the house every six hours, Major was her only protection inside the home.

A burnt orange temperature of 38.4 Celsius spiked on Ian's phone from the back patio, as Major rose, sniffed the air, and came slowly down the steps into the yard towards the synthoid, which—perfectly motionless and odorless—waited safely in the shrubbery.

Major sniffed the ground at the far end of the lilac bushes.

Ian smiled as he watched the telemetry countdown the distance to the growing orange glow from 1300 mm to 400 mm as Major moved down the shrubbery.

The synthoid abruptly reached through the leaves, grabbed Major's snout, and twisted harshly to the right, breaking the dog's neck without a sound. It pulled the body through the bushes and laid it beneath the lilacs. The synthoid stood and slid alongside the fence, moving quickly through the shadows and entering the garage through an unlocked side door. CMOS optical sensors automatically adjusted to the darkness and it found the switch by the door into the house.

When Ian saw the garage door begin to open, he started his pickup truck and pulled up the long driveway and in beside Mrs. Scofield's Mercedes S-Class Sedan. The door closed behind him.

The synthoid was already inside the house, searching.

"So, have you ever been to Senator Scofield's home?" Ian asked Monique.

She stared back with her squinted eyes and gritted her teeth through the gag.

"I did not think so." He grinned. "Shall we go take a look?"

He opened the driver's door and pulled her out by her arm. They stepped into the mudroom and through there into the kitchen. He sat her down at the table. He checked his phone video.

Motherless Children

Ian had downloaded the plans to the Senator's home from the Building Department and loaded it into the synthoid's memory.

The synthoid moved directly to the upstairs master bedroom, its heat sensors locking on the walk-in closet.

She heard nothing as an arm crossed her neck, grabbed the collar of her robe, and pulled. Simultaneously, her right arm was lifted over her head. Moments later she was unconscious from the chokehold.

"There we go." Ian held his phone out to Monique showing her the Senator's wife sprawled unconscious on the floor. "Now, let the games begin."

~~~

Fallen Angels

"You know, Kim is not happy about this." Jake leaned against the passenger window of the Dodge Charger hidden among the odd collection of cars in the DRC Towing lot.

"It's her brother. You know she can't be here for this," Lt. Sands said.

Jake looked inside the car and saw Special Agent Knox in the driver's seat up front and Wilcox sitting in back. "Hey, guys. How's that missing persons thing with De La Croix working out?"

The FBI agents glanced over at Jake. Knox scowled, then looked back through his binoculars through the alleyway at Detective Rick waiting alone in the empty industrial parking lot on East 33rd Street. Wilcox shook his head and fiddled with the controls on the digital recorder.

"I see you invited some new friends along," Jake muttered to Lt. Sands.

"Well, since Rick works for them, we can't exactly ask Internal Affairs to the party. Know what I mean?"

"I guess. Rick's wired, right?"

"Tech gear courtesy of the Feds. Good stuff. They put a couple of snipers on the roofs and brought almost a dozen other agents to help out. Nothing like taking down a corrupt politician, I guess."

"A local one, anyways. Does the Captain know?"

Lt. Sands shook his head. "I took Rick from your place down to the FBI where he spilled his guts. Not sure where the splash zone is going to be on this scene after we collar Corrigan."

"And Wally?"

"Parked back in Exit Alley with EC. Do you really think he's involved?"

"My gut says no. It might be just his hormones talking."

"Amanda?"

Jake shrugged. "So, just you and me?"

"It's the Fed's show now."

"The target is departing Public Square," Wilcox said from the back seat.

"You want eyes on this, right?" Jake whispered at the Lieutenant.

Lt. Sands nodded slightly.

"Then I guess I'll be on my way." Jake put his earbuds in and heard Detective Rick's heavy breathing. *You better calm down, man.*

Jake lightly tapped the rear quarter panel as he walked away and caught Knox looking back over his shoulder. He walked between the old brick industrial buildings down East 38th Street, then turned west on Hamilton Avenue.

As he passed by, Detective Rick stood out in the center of the parking lot behind the Iron Mountain Records Company steel warehouse, kicking at the weeds growing up through the asphalt and looking around at the surrounding buildings.

Jake looked for glints of light from the sniper rifles on the top of the warehouse and the abandoned four-story brick building to the north. He didn't see them, but he knew they were there.

"Target is now six minutes out," said Wilcox over the radio. "Team Alpha?"

"Ready."

"Team Bravo?"

"Ready."

Jake cut behind the elevated railroad tracks to the brick underpass at East 33rd Street. He walked through and stepped back into the tree line along the side of the road, guessing Corrigan would park out on the street for a quick getaway.

"Target turned down East 38th Street…Now left on Hamilton."

Corrigan was following Jake's path around the meeting site.

Five minutes later, an unmarked Crown Vic turned south off Lakeside Road onto East 33rd Street, killing its headlights. It passed the rundown bar, Club 216, slowed to a crawl, then pulled off on the side of the road crunching the gravel.

Jake recognized the Assistant Safety Director from his website photo staring through the driver's side window.

Corrigan looked across the parking lot at Detective Rick, then scanned the rooftops, too. He waited, checking his rear-view mirror, the road ahead, and the parking lot repeatedly.

Jake peeked through the leaves and noticed Detective Rick turn his attention towards the Crown Vic.

Sean Corrigan got out of the car, checking East 33rd Street up and down again. He quietly pushed the driver's door shut. He held a service pistol low against the back of his thigh and slowly stepped across the street.

Jake pulled out his Colt 1911.

Corrigan walked by Jake's hiding spot, heading intently towards Detective Rick.

The Feebs are definitely not going to be happy about this, Jake thought as he quietly slipped out from behind the trees. He watched Corrigan move forward, then crouched and slid along the tree line towards the men.

Corrigan stopped twenty-one feet away from Detective Rick. Corrigan took a deep breath, then let it out slowly. "So, you called this meeting."

"We have to talk."

"About what? How you really screwed things up. Big time."

"Come on, man. You know Jhing Xho was getting close to the money."

"Never should have let that happen. You were supposed to be all over that."

"Easier said than done."

"It was *free money*. The Stein, Baylor insurance made good on it for Jhing."

Detective Rick cleared his throat nervously. "I guess he got greedy."

"Yeah, well, I'm greedy, too. All you had to do was lean on Q and Jake. That's why I approved his consulting contract."

"That Q is slippery."

"*Slippery?*" Corrigan shook his head. "You are Internal Affairs. You deal with slippery all the time."

The two men stared at one another.

Corrigan asked, "So, how is this going to end?"

"What do you mean?"

Corrigan slowly began to move his right arm.

"I'll tell you how this is going to end," Jake said as he stepped out from the tree line. "Corrigan, don't raise your pistol. The snipers will take you down."

"Snipers?"

"On the rooftops." Jake looked at the buildings left and right. "Don't know where exactly, but they are there."

Motherless Children

"You sold me out?" Corrigan asked Detective Rick.

"Show him," Jake said. He pointed at Detective Rick's chest.

Unbuttoning his blue Oxford shirt, he pulled it open to reveal a microphone taped to his chest.

"The Feds are not going to be happy about this," said Jake, "but maybe you should exercise your right to remain silent."

"Son-of-a-bitch—" Corrigan raised his Glock towards Detective Rick.

Jake fired three shots into Corrigan.

As he spun and fell, four more .308 sniper rounds from the Hostage Rescue Team slammed into his body.

"Don't move. And don't…" Jake zipped his fingers over his mouth.

"Why?" Detective Rick asked.

"Kim's my partner." Jake looked down at Corrigan. "And he's a dirtbag."

~~~

Facetime

"I knew you would take this call," Ian said, staring into Mrs. Scofield's phone.

The Senator closed the door on his Capitol office hideaway. "Who are you?"

Ian reversed the camera and held up Mrs. Scofield's iPhone to show the Senator's wife and mistress tied to dining room chairs and gagged. "See them?"

The Senator's face paled as he sat down behind his desk. He coughed to clear his throat. "I do."

"Interesting, isn't it, now: Your wife…" Ian shifted the camera and zoomed in on Mrs. Scofield.

A scowl crossed the craggy old politician's face.

Ian turned the camera to Monique. "…and your lover."

The Senator moaned audibly.

"Yes, yes, yes. I thought so." Ian smiled. "I thought so."

"What do you want?"

"I knew about your son."

"What about him?"

"I know what Mitchell did with the Chinese—and so does she." Ian slid his fingers on the screen into an extreme close-up on Monique's face. "And who he did it for: *you.*"

The Senator clenched his jowls. "Did you kill him?"

"In a way. In a way." Ian zoomed the camera lens out to

show Mrs. Scofield and Monique again. He signaled the synthoid to step out from the darkness by the china cabinet in the back of the room to stand behind the women. Its hands mechanically latched onto their shoulders. Its fingers hydraulically tightened.

Mrs. Scofield winced at it in fear.

"Are you going to kill them?" the Senator asked softly.

"Do you know who those people are?" Ian asked.

"What people?"

"Depraved. That's what they are."

"Who?"

"They prey on young women. That is what they do. I know. I have seen its destruction. First hand." Ian thought about Alicia Walsh and his boss. He took a deep breath, held it for three seconds, then began to exhale. "It must be stopped. Someone has to do it. Someone has to stop it."

"But I had nothing to do with anything like that—"

"Nothing? What about Jhing Xho?"

"Who is that?"

"Yes. Of course, plausible deniability. How convenient."

"Convenient?"

Ian zoomed in on Monique and said to her, "You know who he is. Right? And so did Mitchell. He knew so that the Senator would not have to."

"I do not know who Jhing Xho is."

"He brokers young women—girls, for men like you."

"Me? Ah, I don't know what you mean."

"No?" Ian scanned the camera back to Mrs. Scofield. "You know, though. Don't you."

Mrs. Scofield stared back, then slowly shook her head.

Motherless Children

"Of course, you are all in on it. All of you."
Ian hung up the phone.

~~~

Partners

Jake sat on the edge of the pool table downstairs at the Glick Building, drinking a Shiner Bock. He heard the back door open, then close. He listened for the footsteps but did not recognize them.

Wally stopped at the opposite end of the pool table. He spread his arms out and leaned down on the edge of the table. "Lt. Sands said you shot him."

Jake took a drink of beer. He nodded his head. "I'm sure the FBI. has it all on video."

"Yeah. He said."

"Grab a beer, if you want."

"No…thanks." Wally took a big breath, held it, then exhaled. "Somebody's got to tell Amanda."

"I take it you're the somebody."

"Yeah. I guess I am."

Jake turned around and looked at Wally. "I didn't think the snipers would have saved Rick. But I guess it doesn't really matter one way or the other, does it?"

"No. I guess not." Wally shook his head. "I didn't know he went off the rails. Honest, I didn't."

Jake started to say something but stopped himself.

"A long time. I've known Corrigan a long, long time. Ever since I got assigned to District Three, coming out of the academy.

He was my first partner, you know. I learned a hell of a lot from him."

"And he was your friend."

Wally grimaced. "Yeah."

"There are a lot of gray areas at the edges. So, he got greedy. It can be tempting. And you can't trace Bitcoins—at least that's what Q says."

"I get it. Everybody is, huh? I mean I get greedy sometimes, too. I guess. But him and Rick were leaking information about our cases—about my cases to Jhing Xho. That's just not right."

"So, the money…" Jake stood up and turned to face Wally. "Do you think that's all it was?"

"What do you mean?"

"Corrigan spent a lot of years in District Three. A lot of years covering AsiaTown. What about Jhing's other…businesses?"

"Prostitutes?" Wally scratched the back of his head. "I don't know."

"It seems like a bit more than just running call girls. The four hundred and fifty million dollars was for Jhing and his buddies to buy an island in the Caribbean. Maddie said it has a…well, a checkered past with some billionaire sex maniac."

"I think I'm getting a headache." Wally leaned over and grabbed his head.

"Oh, but wait. There's more. Jhing is getting a shipment from China this week that was arranged by Mitchell Scofield's company."

Wally shook his head.

"And the money…"

"What?" Wally looked up at Jake. "Come on. Out with it."

"Remember on the bridge, the night we took down the Baron?"

Motherless Children

"Yeah?"

"And the blonde orphan girl that ran to Maddie? Q saw her at the bank, converting some of the four hundred and fifty million in Bitcoins into cash."

"Where is she now?"

"Don't know."

"I can't deal with this right now." Wally stood up straight. "I've got to go see Amanda."

"It's almost midnight."

"I can't let her hear find out about this on the news. I've got to tell her, in person."

"I get it."

The front door opened. Kim stepped into the building, then stopped short. "Oh, hey, Wally. What's going on?"

Wally took a deep breath. "I've got to go tell Amanda about her dad."

Kim simply nodded.

"Tomorrow we'll figure all this other stuff with the cases out." Wally turned and headed out back.

Kim and Jake watched him leave.

"I heard you saved my brother's life," Kim whispered to Jake.

"We're partners."

"Really?"

"Of course."

~~~

Kristie

"Who is this?" Kristie from 5 Alive News asked as she grabbed her cell phone off the nightstand and answered the call. "And how did you get this number?"

"Maybe you should just shut up and listen," Ian said.

"Hey, I don't need your—"

"I have Senator Scofield's wife."

"Have?" Kristie pulled the sleep mask off her face. She listened to the silence on the line.

"And his mistress," Ian said. "Kind of convenient."

"Who are you?"

Ian snapped a picture of the women tied to the dining room chairs, then texted it to Kristie. He heard her phone ping. "Do you believe me now?"

Kristie stared at the photo, then put the phone back to her ear. "Where are you?"

"Are you interested?" Ian heard a helicopter's blades approach out over the lake. He walked into the kitchen by the sliding glass door leading to the back patio. In the moonlight, he could make out the orange of a Coast Guard MH-80 Stingray slow, then hover thirty feet up at the water's edge.

"Interested in what?"

"An interview. Just you. On your cell phone."

"Now?"

"No cameramen. No sound guys. No producers. Nobody. Just you. A one-time offer. Now or never."

Kristie thought for a moment.

"Well?" Ian asked.

"Okay."

"I'll text you the address." Ian hung up.

The spotlight on the helicopter crept up off the water and scanned the shoreline.

Ian slipped onto the back patio. He pulled a pistol with a silencer out of his belt and smiled. "Of course. The Senator."

The spotlight methodically searched up the backyard towards the house.

Halfway up to the back patio, Ian fired five quick rounds towards the spotlight on the nose of the helicopter. The silenced poofs of the shots died as they echoed towards the lake.

The jet engine wound up and the helicopter banked to the northwest and quickly climbed.

"Well, she better hurry up," Ian said to himself as he texted the Senator's address to Kristie.

~~~

Jake recognized Kristie's burner phone number. He said to Kim, "I better take this." He answered her call, "This better be good."

"I'm on my way to Bratenahl," Kristie said. "To the Senator's house."

"Okay…"

"Somebody's kidnapped his wife and, evidently, his lover, too."

"Who?"

"Don't know. But he called me—for an interview."

"You can't be serious."

"He certainly seems to be."

"Kristie, you can't go in there."

"Try and stop me." She signaled to exit the Shoreway on Eddy Road. "But maybe a little backup would help. I didn't know who else to call."

"Dammit."

"I'll send you the address. Gotta go." Kristie hung up. She got off the highway and turned north, then back east along Lakeshore Boulevard, watching the addresses until she came up to the Senator's mansion.

She slowed in the empty street, took a deep breath, then pulled into the long driveway. Stopping where it circled around to the front of the house, she texted the address to Jake, then stared at the front door.

Without warning, her car door opened and her arm was locked in a vise-like grip from the synthoid. She was yanked out from behind the driver's seat.

As she gasped, another hand covered her mouth and she was dragged towards the front door.

~~~

Reagan National Airport

Senator Scofield stood at the window of his hideaway, staring at the Capitol Reflecting Pool and sipping a single malt scotch.

"Yes," he answered the knock.

"Excuse me, sir," his Chief-of-Staff opened the door and leaned into the room.

"Come in."

She closed the door behind her, clutching her ever-present leather portfolio. "We've gotten word back from the Coast Guard."

Scofield stared at the Reflecting Pool. "And…"

"They claim shots were fired at their helicopter."

"From my home?"

"Yes, sir."

He downed the last of his scotch.

"I've made NetJets arrangements for you at Reagan National."

"Who?"

"Is that really important now?"

The Senator turned and glared at his Chief-of-Staff.

"Dao Lequ Corporation."

"Jhing Xho." The Senator sighed. "Damn Chinese."

"You will be met at Reagan by a Senior HQ Supervisor and several FBI Agents who will travel with you. A local Hostage Rescue Team is being assembled in Cleveland. You should land at Burke Lakefront shortly before dawn."

"Shots were fired from my house?"

"Yes." The Chief-of-Staff nodded. "Your bags are in the car."

The Senator nodded. He set his empty glass on his desk, then headed downstairs to his limo.

~~~

"You buckled?" Jake asked as he pulled the Mustang out of the back lot behind his building.

"Not my first rodeo," Kim answered.

He headed north.

"What are we going to do when we get there?" Kim asked.

"Not exactly sure." The engine growled as he turned east on Clifton Boulevard and upshifted. "Call EC and tell him to meet us there with Wally."

"What about Sands?"

"Yeah, him, too." Jake's phone rang. He saw Maddie's name on the screen. "Hey, what's wrong? It's like two in the morning."

"The job called and I'm on my way to the airport—heading to Cleveland," Maddie said. "So, what's going on there?"

"You traveling with the Senator?" Jake asked.

"Don't know. Why?"

"Mrs. Scofield's been kidnapped. Along with Monique De La Croix."

"Where?"

"Evidently, inside the Senator's mansion."

"Who?"

"Don't know."

"Wait—how do you know about that?"

"I'm heading there now."

"How do you know?"

"Ah, a long story."

"Yeah, well, they're assembling an HRT."

"Oh, good." Jake looked at Kim and rolled his eyes.

"We should be in Cleveland by five. And don't do anything stupid," Maddie said.

"You know me."

"Just be careful."

~~~

Ian

It took her into the dining room and stood her in front of Ian.

"We are not going to scream, now are we?" Ian asked. He sat ramrod straight in a dining room chair in front of Mrs. Scofield and Monique, still zip-tied to the arms and legs of their chairs. "This residence is quite isolated, so I do not really think it matters—except to severely annoy me."

Kristie shook her head and the synthoid dropped its hand from her mouth.

Kristie looked down at the grip on her arm.

Ian waved his hand and the synthoid released her arm and stepped back. Ian sneered at Kristie.

"What is it?"

"It is the middle of the night and your hair and your makeup are, well, perfect…. and a pressed black pants suit."

"I am a professional."

"Of course. Of course."

"And so now I am here. What do you want to talk about?"

"Sit." Ian motioned towards another chair facing him.

Kristie hesitated, then slowly sat. She folded her hands on her lap, studying Ian's high and tight light brown haircut and clean-shaven face. His pale, ice-blue eyes locked on her gaze.

"Do you know these women?" Ian asked.

"Of course, I have met Mrs. Scofield." She looked at Monique.

"But, I'm sorry, I do not know you."

"Well, perhaps, you should record this."

"I would like to, but…"

Ian nodded at the synthoid.

Unsmiling, it held out her cell phone.

Kristie stared back at the android. "He's one of them, right?"

"One of several."

"One? You mean here?"

"It is really of no matter to you." Ian nodded towards the synthoid. "Take your phone so we can get started."

Hesitantly, Kristie did as she was told.

It gave her a friendly smile and set it gently in her hand.

Staring the synthoid down, she opened the camera app, then turned to Ian. She hit the red record button, adjusted the focus, and pointed it at Ian.

The synthoid stepped back, then turned to face them.

Ian took a deep breath. He nodded slightly at the synthoid, then exhaled a bit. "These women—"

"No. First, who are you?" Kristie asked.

Ian looked at her with disdain. "This is not about me."

"Well, I beg to differ on that. Remember you called me here to interview you. That's my job—and I'm good at it."

He slowly rubbed his chin. "Ian. My name is Ian."

"And what do you do, Ian? For a living?"

"That is not important."

"I think it is."

"I work for the city."

"And do you kidnap women like this on a regular basis? Or is this something new for you?" Kristie gave Ian a wry smile.

He looked up at the ceiling, took another deep breath, then

glared at her. "Of course, we can arrange for you to join them. Tied to your own chair."

Kristie looked over at the synthoid standing to the side with the same friendly smile locked on its face. Unsmiling now, she turned back to Ian and said, "No. This will be just fine."

"Very well. This woman, here," Ian turned to his right and motioned towards Mrs. Scofield, "has been the Senator's wife for—how long is it now? Thirty-five years?".

Her eyes narrowed as she cringed.

"Mrs. Scofield, we talked about this."

She nodded quickly.

"Very faithfully, I would say…even though the Senator has had his share of…indiscretions." Ian turned to the left and waved his hand towards Monique. "One of them being…"

"Is infidelity what this is about? A man's indiscretions? It's an old, old story, my friend."

"Why would Mrs. Scofield allow this? Again…and again…and again?"

"Maybe they have an arrangement. It has been known to happen—especially with politicians. They love their power and who are we to judge?"

"Oh, but it goes far, far beyond that."

"And how is that?"

"At least Ms. De La Croix is of…legal age. Not all of them were."

Kristie looked at the Senator's wife. "Is this true?"

Mrs. Scofield took a deep breath and looked down at her knees.

Kristie glanced sideways at Monique.

"I did not intend to kidnap Ms. De La Croix, you know. It was an…" Ian looked into Monique's eyes. He grinned maliciously.

"…impulse, you see. I could not resist myself. You understand, right?"

"No. As a matter of fact, I do not."

"Or I could have let her be killed, like the others."

"Others?"

Ian smiled. "We will get to that."

Kristie asked Monique. "Have you been—I mean, are you…okay?"

"Of course, she is *okay*. I am not a pervert."

"Oh, no. Of course not." Kristie frowned at Ian. "Why would I think that?"

Ian narrowed his ice-blue eyes on Kristie. "Do you know of her business? With the Senator and his son?"

"Mitchell? Did you kill him?"

"He imports certain items from overseas."

"What items?"

"And, of course, the *Big Guy*…" Ian nodded his head back towards Mrs. Scofield, "…always got his *fair share.*"

"A United States Senator? Corrupted? So what. Another old, old story. It's politics, my friend."

"It is more than corruption. There is a darkness there. An evil darkness. And she…" Ian got up and stepped around behind Monique. He grabbed the hair on the back of her neck. "…*helps* the Senator."

"Hey, you don't need to do that," Kristie growled lowly.

"No. You do not understand." Ian pulled Monique's head all the way back and smiled down at her. "Have you ever heard of Alicia Walsh?"

Kristie shook her head. "No. I have not. Who is Alicia?"

Ian released his grip on Monique and paced back and forth

behind the women. "There are men, like the Senator, who believe somehow they are above it all. That their needs are all that matter."

"Who is Alicia Walsh?"

"I told you. I have seen it with my own eyes. Her father—it was unbearable. And what did the police do? What did the prosecutors do? A slap on the wrist, thanks to his lawyer. Well, I showed them."

"Them?"

"This other world that lives all around us. That no one pays any attention to. It sucks the life out of them all."

"You killed him?"

"Oh, no. Not me. I did not have to." Ian stopped pacing and looked at the synthoid.

Kristie turned and pointed her phone at the synthoid with the same friendly smile on its face. "This one?"

"And others like it."

"How many have you killed?"

"Mr. Whistler was the first. He thought he was meeting another…young girl, late at night in the park. After he ruined Alicia. He is quite fond of them, you know. And shares that interest with many other sick people…like the Senator."

Kristie grimaced.

"Yes. At his Bistro. Iris and Dolly's in Ohio City. Have you been there?"

"No, I, um…" Kristie bit her lower lip. "But I have heard of it."

"Yes. Of course, you have." Ian shook his head. He pulled a photo from a manila folder on the long dining room table and handed it to Kristie.

She saw the Senator sitting at a table with his painted-on

political smile. Paul Whistler stood behind him with his hand on the Senator's shoulder. On the wall behind them was a black-and-white movie poster of Jodie Foster from *Taxi Driver*, leaning against a telephone pole in short shorts, a small black tube top, and a floppy hat.

"Alicia was not much older than her: Iris. There in the picture." Ian sighed. "And they just let Whistler get off scot-free—maybe because of his friends. Maybe *The Big Guy*, perhaps. No?"

"And what did you do about it?"

"It is nothing really. A trade I learned in the Army, being *all I can be.*" Ian smiled. "Somebody has to make their *warriors* strong and ready. And that person was me."

"Whistler? And Mitchell, and…"

"It is all woven together. So tightly, no one else can see it. Or maybe some people just do not want to see it do they, Mrs. Scofield?"

She closed her eyes tightly.

"Of course, there was the despicable lawyer in Little Italy. And two of his other scumbag clients." Ian smiled broadly. "You see, Kyle, we are not all helpless."

"Who is Kyle?"

Ian shrugged. "It is of little matter."

"And right here? Right now? What is going on?" Kristie asked. "With these women?"

Ian smiled.

"Is this meant to punish the Senator?"

"Oh, he knows. He knows for sure what will be coming his way. In the end, they all know their fate."

"But isn't he in Washington right now?"

"He and I have spoken and he certainly knows I mean business."

"They won't let him get within a mile of this place now."

"We will see what happens. No? Anyway, we have our interview." Ian stepped over to Kristie and took her phone from her hand. He stopped the recording. He looked at the synthoid and said, "You can stop recording now, too."

Kristie stared up at the synthoid. "And…and what about me?"

"Now." Ian nodded at the synthoid, which quickly moved behind her and locked her arms to the chair.

"No!"

"We shall see," Ian smiled as he zip-tied her arms to the chair. "We shall see."

~~~

Little Fires Everywhere

Jake killed the headlights and slowed the Mustang to a crawl as he pulled past the long driveway leading towards the Senator's front door. The metal gate was not closed and he saw Kristie's car with the driver's door still open. "Yeah, I'm not liking this."

"Holy mackerel. That place is huge," Kim said, gawking at the Senator's three-story, brick mansion slowly being swallowed by ivy. "So, now what?"

Jake pulled the car to the far end of the lot beyond the stone wall behind the sidewalk where he parked across the street. He turned off the engine. "I guess we investigate."

"Just us?"

"EC and Wally should be here soon."

"Maybe we should wait."

"I'm really thinking that's not such a good idea." He shook his head. "Besides, we're detectives, remember?"

"Yeah…but…"

"Come on." Jake got out and walked around back to open the trunk.

Kim shook her head. She slid out the passenger door, stepped around, and looked down at the small arsenal of weapons, ammunition, and gear inside. "What the…"

"Be prepared. Right?"

"Seriously?"

"You got a vest on?"

"Ah, no." Kim shook her head. "I was off-duty when I came by earlier."

He handed her a Kevlar vest. "Here. It's Maddie's."

"What about you?"

"I'm not stupid." Jake grabbed another bulletproof vest out of the trunk and strapped it on with Velcro.

"Okay, so what's the plan?"

Jake handed her a shotgun and a canvas bag of shells. "First, load this up."

Kim began pushing shells into the gun. "And then?"

Jake strapped an eM&P to the outside of his leg. He unholstered it to charge the pistol. The gun whined, then beeped three times. Jake confirmed the green light at the bottom of the red dot sight and re-holstered it. He handed Kim a CRM-114 ePD scanner. "You know how to use this?"

"I went through the training."

Jake sighed. "But do you know how to use it?"

"I did just fine on the practicals."

"No real world?"

Kim's shoulders sank. "No."

"If he's got any synthoids in there, we have to neutralize them fast."

"I'll be fine." Kim scowled at Jake.

"Sure. No worries. I trust you." Jake handed her a pair of ThirdEye LE-XR augmented reality glasses.

"We're on our own. No tech back up. Remember that." Jake put on his AR glasses and turned them on. "You got the heads-up display?"

Kim powered up her glasses. "Got it."

He felt for his Colt 1911 on his right hip, then grabbed a 277 Sig Fury rifle. "Okay. We'll go down the far side along the wrought iron fence to the waterline, then come up from the back."

Jake quietly closed the trunk and started across the street with Kim following. Just then EC and Wally pulled in behind the Mustang.

"What's up?" Wally asked, killing the headlights.

Jake came back over to the driver's window. "That's Kristie's car in the driveway. Looks like she's been grabbed and pulled inside."

"Think we should wait for SWAT?" EC asked.

"I don't think we have time," Jake said. "We're going down to the water and come up from the back. You guys secure the front. Good?"

"No problem," Wally said.

Jake and Kim moved along the outside of the fence in the neighbor's yard down to the lakeshore. They crossed the sandy beach, worked their way around the small boathouse, and climbed up the rise. They lay shoulder-to-shoulder facing back up towards the house.

"There," Jake said. "Through the sliding door."

They could see a shadow moving past an inside doorway behind the curtains.

"I count three," Kim said, scanning the interior of the mansion with a heat sensor on the ePD scanner. "No. Four. Three sitting. Two are close together. One pacing."

"One of those might be Kristie."

"And Mrs. Scofield, De La Croix, and the kidnapper."

"No synthoids?"

"Not in the house."

Jake scanned the first-floor windows through the scope on his Sig Sauer rifle. "I don't see anything through the other windows. They must be deep inside the house. That's good. You go up the left and I'll take the right. Let's figure out what's going on."

Kim and Jake split up and, crouching, moved slowly up along the bushes and shrubbery along each side of the lawn.

Jake came across the body of Major in the lilac bushes with his head twisted back around. He double-blinked and flashed an image over to Kim's glasses.

"That's not good," Kim whispered to herself.

"What do you see now?" Jake asked over the secure ThirdEye com link.

"Definitely four. Looks like two rooms deep—Wait, the temps show a much cooler human form in the garage—must have been shielded behind the cars. There it is. I've got an RF ping. It's coming back into the house. Thermals show it's got something in each hand."

"What is it carrying?"

"Can't tell. Heading upstairs now." Kim whispered. "On the second floor now…oh, no."

"What?"

"Cans. Splashing it around like…like it's some kind of accelerant."

"Gas?"

"Yeah…I'd guess."

Jake asked EC and Wally, "Did you guys hear that?"

Wally clicked his transmit button twice.

"Now what?" EC asked.

~~~

Ian looked down the hallway to see the synthoid step off the rear stairway to return to the garage for more jerrycans.

"So, do you even have a plan at all?" Kristie asked. "Or are you just going to let the snipers end all of this?"

"Suicide by cop?" Ian looked over. "Oh no…no. I'll be long gone before the rest of the party shows up."

"And exactly how is that?"

"I don't need to go out the front door. There is a boathouse out back. You, on the other hand…"

"Me?"

"…will see the show and see how the Senator gets what he so well deserves."

"And what is that?"

Ian walked over and hopped up to sit on the dining room table. "To me belongeth vengeance, and recompense; Their foot shall slide in due time."

"Seriously? What is that? Shakespeare? Bible verses?"

"Deuteronomy."

The synthoid passed by again in the hallway and went upstairs, carrying two more cans of gasoline.

Kristie looked up at the sound of the synthoid's steps moving around upstairs. "What is he doing?"

Ian smiled. "Oh, you will see soon enough."

"That smells like…"

"Yes. Gasoline." Ian smiled. "Get the picture?"

"But what—why?"

"Enablers—all of you." He pointed at Mrs. Scofield. "You knew. All along, didn't you?"

She narrowed her eyes at Ian.

"And, of course, his mistress…and business partner, over

here." Ian waved his other arm towards De La Croix. "Tell me, did Mitchell know about your…*extracurricular* activities with his father?"

Defeated, Monique turned her head to stare out the sliding glass door in the back.

"No, I did not think so."

"But why me?" Kristie asked. "You got your interview and—"

"You knew about them…about them all, right?" Ian hopped down off the dining room table. He went over and leaned down on the arms of Kristie's chair. He put his face directly into hers. "The Senator…the rich businessmen…the famous movie stars? The artists and musicians. Right?"

"What—but I—?"

"All of them. You knew about all of the depravity and the corruption. And what did you say? I think it was, 'It's an old, old story.' That is what you told me earlier, right?"

"But—"

"You knew all along about Iris and Dolly's Bistro in Ohio City." Ian picked up the picture of Whistler and the Senator again and waved it in her face. "You knew what went on there. And who exactly went there. Everybody did, didn't they?"

"I heard things—"

"And you said?" Ian glared into her eyes. "Something? Anything?"

"I-I-I couldn't prove what was happening."

"Oh, no. Of course not." Ian stood up straight. "The only thing necessary for the triumph of evil…is that good men do nothing."

"These are powerful people—"

"But you knew."

Motherless Children

~ ~ ~

"Quick, what's the floor plan?" Jake asked.

EC closed his eyes to remember back to the day he, Lt. Sands, and Wally notified the Senator and his wife about the murder of Mitchell. "Big entryway. Circular stairs up. Music room to the left. Living room to the right. Came down a hallway. Maybe a great room in back. Lots of windows. Turned down another hallway to the left which leads back to the Senator's study at the far west end of the house looking out on the lake. There was another stairway back there going up. That's all we saw."

"The synthoid's moved to another room upstairs," Kim said. "Another can."

"Just one synthoid, right?" Jake asked.

"So far."

"We're going to need a distraction to get inside," Jake said.

"Maybe a friendly knock on the front door," Wally said. "It is three-thirty in the morning. That would distract me."

"Well, if that's gas upstairs," EC said, "SWAT definitely can't use CS."

"So we have to get in there. I'll try the side door on the garage," Jake said. "EC, grab the bolt cutters out of my trunk and see if you can find the power drop into this place."

"Will do," EC said.

Jake moved to the corner of the house, then entered through the same door where the synthoid first came in. "Where's the droid?"

"Still upstairs," Kim said.

"Okay, you watch the back."

"Got it." Kim moved to take cover behind a stone fireplace

chimney at the edge of the patio, aiming the shotgun at the sliding glass door and checking the screen of the ePD.

"Six hundred horsepower—that corrupt son-of-a-bitch," Jake paused and muttered to himself before he slid past a velocity yellow Maserati MC20. He noticed a white pickup truck labeled with a red-white-and-blue Cleveland city logo on the door, parked between a Mercedes S-Class Sedan and a Cadillac Escalade. In the bed of the truck were six more five-gallon cans of gasoline.

"Wally, you on the front door?"

"Thirty minutes or it's free," Wally said.

"EC?"

"Here. Just call it," EC said.

"Synthoid's moving downstairs again," Kim said.

Jake war-gamed scenarios in his head, whether to take the synthoid down in the garage by himself where he only had one clear shot with his eM&P at the doorway or isolate it back upstairs, but with more gasoline. He was certain the Three Laws chip was disabled and cutting the power would have no effect on the android's visual capabilities…but what would the kidnapper do with the women when the lights went out?

"Wally, when I say 'go,' beat on the front door then get inside somehow—maybe through a front window if you can. We have to get to the women fast."

"Shock and awe, man." Wally slid up behind the brick wall on the hinge side of the front door.

"EC give it a three-count, then cut the lines. Get around back and inside with Kim," Jake said. "She's got a lock on where the women are."

Jake moved quickly behind the driver's door on the Escalade. Drawing his eM&P, he set the discharge to 65% to give himself a quicker second shot if needed. He flipped his AR glasses into full thermal mode, grabbed his flashlight, leaned against the Escalade door, and listened.

~~~

Kristie saw Mrs. Scofield's head and shoulders sag. Monique stared blankly through the doorway into the great room towards the windows into the backyard.

Ian paced with slow steady steps back and forth beside the long dining room table.

The synthoid came down the stairs again and passed by on its way back to the garage.

"Make these the last cans," Ian said, stopping at the doorway.

It paused at the dining-room door.

Ian smiled cruelly at Kristie. "I think it's about time for me to move on. Don't you know?" He looked back at the synthoid. "You know what to do then."

The synthoid nodded. Its harsh, dark eyes burned into Kristie.

She shuddered and looked away, back at Monique seeing her head had turned a bit to the side, her blank gaze now focused on something outside.

Monique winked twice at Kristie. She glanced quickly at Ian, then motioned with her eyes towards the great room.

Kristie quickly looked back to Ian and asked, "And...and what is it that you have in mind for the Senator?"

"Hmm...simply put, hellfire."

All of the women turned in fear towards Ian.

He smiled.

"But they'll never let him come here," Kristie said.

"No. Certainly not. But he will see his home, his life…his loves…burn—burn to ashes. And then…"

Mrs. Scofield pulled at her zip ties, cutting her skin.

"Then?"

"Go on and finish up," Ian said to the synthoid, which nodded and headed towards the garage. "You do realize, this android is not the only one out there."

Suddenly there was a loud banging on the front door.

Ian pulled out his pistol, moved quickly to the hallway, and fired five shots at the front door. He came back into the dining room shooting Mrs. Scofield in the temple, splattering Monique with droplets of blood.

As he pulled the trigger, Kristie kicked him in the crotch from behind and he tumbled to his knees.

All the lights went out.

A shotgun blast shattered the glass on the sliding door.

Hearing the synthoid coming downstairs, Jake slid forward to look around the front grill of the Escalade.

It stopped and he waited, wondering what was going on. The eM&P erratically flashed yellow with less than a 50% frequency lock on the droid's Gyro & Mobility Chip.

Jake finally heard the door handle turn and open.

"Now, Wally—*GO!*"

Wally pounded hard on the front door, then took cover behind the brick wall on the front of the mansion.

The synthoid stopped, turning towards the front entryway as Ian fired his pistol.

Jake stood and leaned on the Escalade hood, closing his eyes to avoid the green glare in his night vision glasses from the light behind the synthoid. He strobed his flashlight at the door to temporarily blind its optical sensors and fired his eM&P.

The lights behind the synthoid went out as EC cut the power lines into the house.

Jake ducked back down behind the Cadillac, moving towards the tailgate, while his eM&P whined as it recharged.

Jake heard shotgun blasts, then, above, a loud detonation.

Ian put his left hand down lifting himself gingerly to his feet, raising his pistol back towards Kristie.

Kim fired three rapid shots into Ian's center mass, spinning his body around and slamming him hard, face-first into the far wall, smearing the white paint with half a rainbow of blood. *"Stop! Police!"*

The shockwave of an explosion knocked Kim off her feet. Flames erupted down the back stairway and into the hall.

EC followed her in with his Glock drawn, scanned the dining room, saw the blood, and Ian down on the floor. He helped Kim to her feet. "You okay?"

She shook the cobwebs from her head. "Yeah. Yeah—where's Jake?"

"The garage I guess."

"Get them out of here."

"Right." EC flipped open his SOG-TAC knife to cut Kristie and Monique free.

Kim racked the slide on her Remington 870 shotgun as she headed towards the garage.

Jake got behind the Escalade tailgate. He listened and heard the synthoid shuffle into the garage, its mobility disabled by his blast, relentlessly scanning the garage—optically, aurally, thermally, and seismically searching for him—no doubt focused on triangulating the high-pitched whine of his pistol.

The eM&P flashed green again. Jake slid the phaser to 100%. He dropped to his belly and crawled under the middle of the Escalade.

In the narrow space beneath the cars, he watched the feet of the synthoid move towards the garage door between the pickup truck and the Mercedes. It stopped at the bed of the pickup, then moved around the tailgate, splashing gasoline from a can on the floor.

At the door into the garage, Kim crouched and scanned in across the rows of cars. Through the windows of the pickup truck, she saw the synthoid pick up a can of gasoline, but her aim was blocked by the cab.

The synthoid limped up between the pickup truck and the Escalade, emptying the first can of gas. It reached into the pickup for another.

Kim moved in at the front of the garage around the Mercedes and the pickup truck, aiming at the synthoid's green glowing silhouette in her AR goggles.

Jake moved the eM&P to his left hand, drew his colt 1911, and flipped off the safety, waiting for the synthoid to move closer.

Gasoline splashed on his ThirdEye glasses and into his

nose. He refliexively coughed.

A shotgun blast echoed in the garage.

Jake aimed his 1911 point-blank at the ankle of the synthoid, firing all eight rounds, shattering its ankle and sweeping it off its feet. Another shotgun blast deafened him.

With its pupils dilated, the deep black eyes of the synthoid were naught but dark holes in his night vision, staring him down as its hand reached for his throat.

Jake aimed his eM&P at the chest of the synthoid where all of the command, control, and biological microchips were located, and pulled the trigger.

The synthoid spasmed.

Kim emptied the last of her shells into the synthoid's head.

Jake was splattered with Dermaloy skin and fragments of composite bone.

Flames burned through the ceiling showering sparks down onto the Maserati's hood, scorching the paint.

The garage door opened behind the Escalade began crawling up its tracks.

"You know, we might want to get the hell out of here," Wally shouted as he manually pulled the door up.

Kim got down on her knees and looked beneath the Escalade. "You okay?"

"Yeah, but Wally's right. Let's blow this pop stand."

"Huh?"

Wally grabbed Kim by the collar and pulled her up and outside into the driveway.

Jake slid himself from under the Escalade and ran out as

the ceiling beams collapsed.

"Where's Kristie?" Jake asked.

"EC got her out the back," Kim said.

They watched the flames climb out the upstairs windows into the night.

"Holy mackerel…" Kim said.

The SWAT team finally arrived. The fire trucks came.

But the flames ferociously consumed the mansion, collapsing it on the bodies of Ian and Mrs. Scofield.

~~~

Burke Lakefront Airport

The Gulfstream G-9 touched down on runway two-four right and taxied to Signature Aviation. The Senator, accompanied by the Senior HQ Supervisor and his Chief-of-Staff, deplaned and headed inside, followed by the rest of the FBI agents from Washington DC.

Maddie peeled off on the tarmac to call Jake but got his voicemail.

At five in the morning, the lobby was deserted, except for a line boy behind the desk, a pilot napping under his cap on a couch by the windows, and two waiting local FBI agents standing by the front entryway.

The FBI huddled together and conferred in low tones near the entrance. Out front, a parade of black Chevy Suburbans idled.

The Chief-of-Staff excused herself to make a phone call.

The Senator looked around the lobby, waiting impatiently. He walked to the window and gazed out at the Gulfstream, shaking his head.

Maddie came inside, looked around, and sensed something was wrong. She walked quickly towards her fellow agents.

Behind her, the pilot rose suddenly, went to the Senator, and grabbed his neck. It lifted the Senator off his feet and hydraulically clamped the carotid arteries closed.

Halfway to the huddle of agents, Maddie heard the commotion, turned, and instinctively drew her Glock.

The Senator lost consciousness.

She ran towards them, firing into the synthoid's center mass.

It absorbed her bullets and simply squeezed harder.

Maddie lowered her shoulders and smashed into the synthoid, crashing the three of them through the plate glass window onto the tarmac.

Maddie rolled and got up on her knees, trying to clear her head.

The synthoid ran north, escaping across the runways.

Ineffectually, she emptied the rest of her rounds at it, then sat back on her knees.

She looked down at the Senator, but, clearly, he was dead.

The Warehouse

Two in the morning. Jake sat up against the headboard in his bed, thinking how Q was still luckless in tracking down the Baron's four hundred and fifty million in cryptocurrency. Kristie slept against his chest.

His iPhone dinged with a text message from Kim: *1840 East 40th Street. You need to come.*

Right now?

Yes.

Jake gently woke Kristie. "Hey…I have to go."

"Huh? What?" She dug her head into his shoulder. "No. You can't."

"It's been almost a week."

"I know…I know…but—but I can't. Not yet."

"It's okay. Stay as long as you want. But this is work."

Kristie scowled, rolling over and burying herself in the blankets. "Stupid work."

Jake kissed the back of her head, then dressed, armed himself, and drove to AsiaTown.

~~~

He parked the Mustang in the middle of East 40th Street, outside the yellow crime scene tape stretched out in front of the red brick warehouse building, scalloped by the red and blue flashing lights of three police cruisers.

Kim stood at the steps leading up to the front door. She waved him over.

Jake showed his badge and logged into the crime scene. "What do we have?"

"Your friend, Jhing Xho."

"Dead?"

"Come on in and take a look." Kim led Jake down a long hallway that opened into a large warehouse. They stood behind CSI technicians taking pictures of a body on the floor, Jhing Xho. "Look at the grip marks on his neck. Strangled. Sound familiar?"

"DNA?"

"Nothing, besides his."

"Where are his bodyguards?"

"MIA."

Jake noticed a synthoid sitting in a nearby chair. He pointed and asked, "What's this?"

"Puff's got the locking bolt in it. Looks like our strangler. He'll know when he downloads the memory."

"And this place?"

"Registered to Jhing's consortium." Kim shook her head. "And…"

"What?"

"Over this way. Remember those shipments coming in from LA and Vancouver? Well, they're here. And you're not going to like it. Remember the Fourth Law?"

"Yeah. Yeah, I do."

"Between five and maybe fourteen years old. Girls *and boys.*" Kim lifted the lid on a coffin-like container. Inside, a naked, red-headed female synthoid, maybe seven or eight years old, was locked in place with styrofoam around her head, shoulders, hips, and ankles. Its dark brown, doe-eyes gazed invitingly up at the ceiling. "Looks like they were getting them ready to move them to that island in the Caribbean."

"So Jhing's murder…is this our case?"

"If you want it."

Jake took a deep breath, then headed back down the hall and outside again.

Kim followed. "We just have to talk to Lt. Sands."

They stepped out from under the crime scene tape.

"Call him." Jake looked north and saw a black Denali pull out slowly from Commerce Street. Through the open rear window, he noticed the smile on the face of a slender, blonde teenager…*Amy.*"

The Denali turned towards the lake and sped away.

Thank you for reading my story.

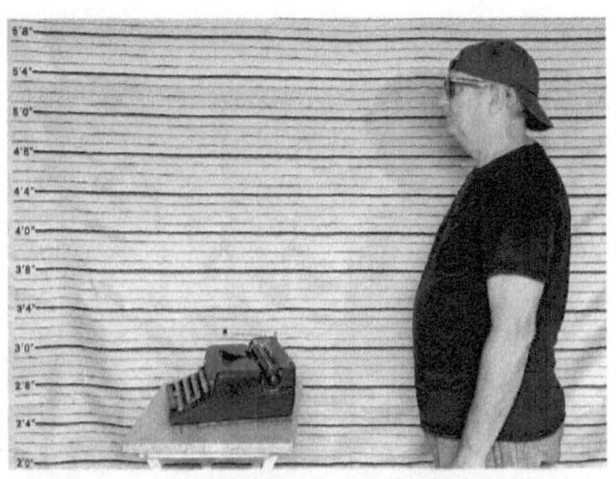

About M.T. Bass

M.T. Bass lives, writes, flies, and plays music in Mudcat Falls, USA.

www.MTBass.net

Murder by Munchausen Sci-Fi Thriller Book #1
Available in Paperback, eBook, & Audiobook

Artificial Intelligence? *Fuhgeddaboudit!*

Artificial Evil has a name…*Munchausen.*

When androids are reprogrammed into hit men, detectives of the Artificial Crimes Unit repo the AnSub and track down the hackers. Partners Jake and EC's case of an "extra-judicial" divorce settlement takes a nasty turn with DNA from a hundred-year-old murder in Boston and a signature that harkens back to the very first serial killer ever in London.

www.MTBass.net

**Murder by Munchausen Sci-Fi Thriller Book #2
Available in Paperback, eBook, & Audiobook**

It was the case of a lifetime…but then it went sideways on her. The serial killer Maddie put behind bars might have been crazy but it turns out he was innocent, and now she finds herself hunting robot killers in the Artificial Crimes Unit. Worse yet, she's partnered up with Jake, her former lover.

When androids are hacked and reprogrammed into hit men, Maddie and Jake investigate and track down the hackers. But now, an evil genius is using droids to recreate the infamous Jack the Ripper murders.

www.MTBass.net

Murder by Munchausen Sci-Fi Thriller Book #3
Available in Paperback, eBook, & Audiobook

Now unleashed, the "Baron" is resurrecting history's notorious serial killers, giving them a second life in the bodies of hacked and reprogrammed Personal Assistant Androids, then turning them loose to terrorize the city. While detectives Jake and Maddie of the police department's Artificial Crimes Unit scramble to stop the carnage with the Baron's arrest, the cyberpunk head of the Counter IT Section, Q, struggles to de-encrypt his mad scheme to infect world data centers with a virus that represents a collective cyber unconsciousness of evil.

www.MTBass.net

White Hawk Aviation Adventure Stories #1
Available in Paperback & eBook

Hollywood, 1950 — Former P-51 fighter pilot A. Gavin Byrd is on location for a movie shoot, when he gets a call from the police that his older brother, a prominent Beverly Hills plastic surgeon, has been found dead on his boat. The Lieutenant in charge of the investigation is ready to close the case as a suicide from the start, but "Hawk" doesn't buy it and decides to find out what really happened for himself.

With help from a former starlet ex-girlfriend, a friendly police sergeant whose life was saved in the war by his brother and a nosy Los Angeles Times reporter, Hawk's search for the truth takes him through cross-fire, dog fights and mine fields in Hollywood, Beverly Hills, Burbank and Las Vegas, and leads him into some of the darker corners of his brother's patient files and private life that he never knew existed.

www.MTBass.net

White Hawk Aviation Adventure Stories #2
Available in Paperback & eBook

"There are only two types of aircraft: fighters and targets."
~Doyle 'Wahoo' Nicholson, USMC

Sweating it out in the former Belgian Congo as a civil war mercenary, with Sparks turning wrenches on his T-6 Texan, Hawk splits his time flying combat missions and, back on the ground, sparring with Ella, an attractive young missionary doctor, in the sequel to My Brother's Keeper.

www.MTBass.net

Available in Paperback, eBook & Audiobook

Griffith Crowe, the "fixer" for a Chicago law firm, falls for his current assignment, Helena Nicholson, the beautiful heir of a Tech Sector venture capitalist who perished in a helicopter crash leaving her half a billion dollars, a Learjet 31, and unsavory suspicions about her father's death. As he investigates, the ex-Navy SEAL crosses swords with Helena's step-brother, the Pentagon's Highlands Forum, and an All-Star bad guy somebody has hired to stop him. When Griff finds himself on the wrong side of an arrest warrant he wonders: Is he a player or being played?

Lawyers and Lovers and Guns…Oh, my!

www.MTBass.net

Available in Paperback & eBook

People ask me where I get the ideas for my books. In this case, I recall reading about Alaska bush pilots for fun. I must have watched *Animal House* and *Treasure of the Sierra Madre* around that time and…a few months later—Eureka! The words for the prologue and first chapter just started spilling out of my head. ("Clean up on aisle five.")

Seriously, what could go wrong? *Love & Betrayal…Murder & Mayhem…Friendship & Double-Crossing Partners in Pursuit of Buried Treasure…*

www.MTBass.net

Available in Paperback & eBook

Kansas City, 1965 — Y.T. Erp, Jr. can't wait to leave for college at the University of California, Berkeley to escape not only the work, but especially all the phlegm-brained idiots at his father's aerospace company. Leaving behind a pregnant auburn-haired cheerleader, a sensuous red-headed siren plotting to usurp his familial ties, and his two best friends—one who ends up in Vietnam and the other in the Weather Underground—his "trip" on the wild side of the Generation Gap takes him from the psychedelic scene of Haight-Ashbury to the F.B.I.'s Ten Most Wanted list. Meanwhile, his father is consumed by the task of managing his unmanageable corporate team in the quest to help fulfill a President's challenge to "land a man on the moon."

www.MTBass.net

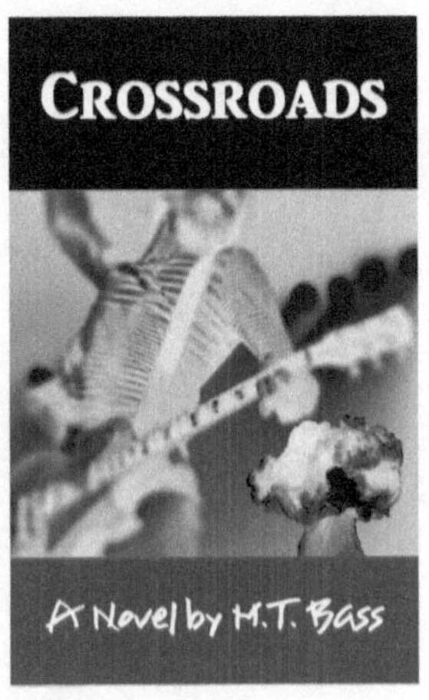

Available in eBook

Cleveland, 1977 — Grappling with a foreign policy crisis, the U.S. Government targets a hapless rock-'n'-roller as a Russian spy in a classic case of mistaken identity for an innocent, 'Wrong Man' hero…or *is he?*

Think of an unholy fictional union between the Rolling Stones and Alfred Hitchcock's *North by Northwest*.

Unlike any novel you have ever read, this one has a soundtrack. After all, a story whose characters are musicians should have…well…*music*. Right?

www.MTBass.net

Available in eBook

Lodging — bending of the stalk of a plant (stalk lodging)
or the entire plant (root lodging)

While World War II engulfs every nation on the globe, Rebecca and her high school friend Sarah can only dream of escaping a dreary, wind-blown existence in western Kansas, until their boring, stodgy old hometown fills with handsome young men learning to fly Army Air Corps bombers known as *Liberators*, and their lives are suddenly filled with temptation and, perhaps, true love.

www.MTBass.net

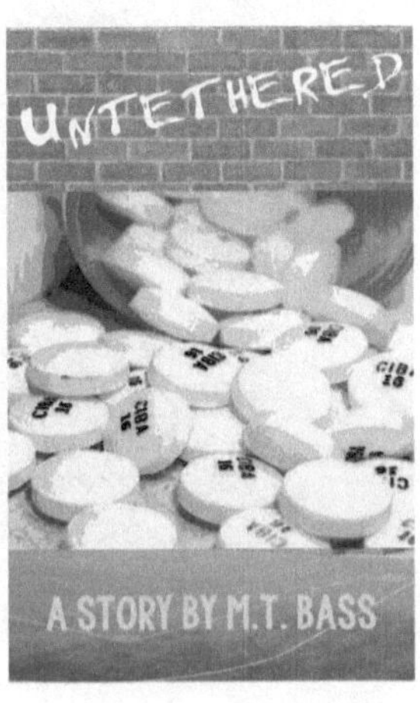

Available in eBook

At District High School #6241, Connor wants only to get close to Liz, the cheerleader whose locker is just across the hall, and forget the suicide of his father in jail, but his family's dark past and a rebellious nature force him to the fringes of student social circles and into an unlikely alliance to fight back against a tyranny of conformity.

www.MTBass.net

Available in eBook

The collected songs and verse of M.T. Bass

www.MTBass.net